"Schaeffer?" Melissa bought the land fro this carving in the haylo named Schaeffer and an axe. It was a lot like the Lizzie Borden rhyme you'd recite while jumping rope."

"Jesus God, I'd forgotten about that!" Ida exclaimed. "I can't believe it's still there! Wow, Tommy carved it up there in the early Sixties!" Melissa stared at Ida quizzically. "Well, it's a long story," Ida said.

"If you've got lots of tea, I've got time." Melissa smiled.

"Oh, alright. But, you ain't squeamish or nothin', are ya?" Ida asked.

A FRESH START

BY SOMER CANON

CHAPTER ONE

The unpacking was going swimmingly until she happened upon a piece of her "before" life, and her stomach knotted up. It was an old, chipped mug that had belonged to a diner that Kyle's family had owned back in the 1940s. Why had she agreed to keep all of his family's crap in the divorce?

She knew the answer. These were things that, yes, belonged to Kyle's family, but they were also keepsakes for her children. Her and Kyle's children. Kyle's mother had begged Melissa to keep some of these cheap but priceless trinkets in the family. Since Kyle was living in an apartment with his mistress... No, she was his girlfriend now. The divorce had been finalized and she could no longer in fairness be called "the mistress." Since they lived together in a small apartment and the girlfriend wasn't fond of old things and clutter, it fell on Melissa to be the keeper of the family's more valued trinkets. She could feel the sour look on her face as she looked down at the stupid mug. She thought briefly about packing away all of the Caan family heirlooms that she'd been saddled with, but these things had all found comfortable places in her cabinets and life. Needing to do something to make herself feel better, she flipped the bird at the mug and said a few choice words to it before placing it gently in her china hutch.

Melissa abandoned her unpacking for the time being and walked out onto her large front porch and sat heavily on the long porch swing. She began swinging slowly and lazily, taking in the quiet and beautiful April morning. She could hear her boys in their new rooms, talking to each other through the walls and playing with toys. Slowly, she felt the anxiety start to melt away from her middle and she began to relax.

She heard the screen door creak open and she turned her head to see Dumb-Dumb walking out to join her. The dog was another thing of Kyle's that she got stuck keeping after the divorce. Apartments in the big city could sometimes be sticklers about tenants keeping big dogs, and Kyle had guilted her, saying that the boys loved the dog. Of course, his name wasn't originally Dumb-Dumb. Kyle had named him and Melissa couldn't stand the highly specified name. Calling him Dumb-Dumb was one of the nicer names she gave him and her boys had found it amusing.

"What do you think, Dumb-Dumb?" she asked the dog, looking down at him. His tail thumped lightly on the wooden planks of the porch and he grunted at her.

Her eyes caught on the old red barn that had been on the property. She had walked through it briefly before she bought the land, but had never really looked around. The chain on the swing squeaked as she got up and started down the porch steps. She heard Dumb-Dumb's tags jingle as he got up and followed her. She walked down the long driveway and through the grass, relaxing further as the nature around her blew away her previous annoyance. The rusted latch on the huge double doors on the barn gave her a little bit of trouble, but she eventually got it to open. She swung one of the doors outward and inhaled deeply. The barn retained the sweet smell of hay and large farm animals. It was warm and light in the huge empty space. She walked around slowly, looking at the rusted chains that hung from the walls. When she saw the rough ladder that led to the hayloft she gave it a good shake, decided it was still sturdy, and made her way to the top. The hayloft was dusty and it looked as if some bats and other critters had made homes up there. Melissa made a mental note to call an exterminator and have the barn thoroughly cleaned of all uninvited visitors. She walked to the large door at the front, the one where the hay would be put in via pulleys, and opened it, letting the sunshine in. The barn was in fantastic shape. The realtor had told her that it had been raised in the 1940s or 50s. By the hay door, she noticed words carved into the wood. She leaned closer and mouthed the words as she read them.

Thomas Shchaeffer done got an axe
And buried it in his two kids' backs
Took a break and ate some bread
And took that axe to Liddy's head.

"Whoa," Melissa said, running her hands over the rough wood, feeling the crude etching against the pads of her fingers.

"MOM!" her seven year-old son, Logan, called.

"I'm in the barn!" she yelled out the hay door.

"Can I come up there?" Logan called from outside of the barn.

"Yeah sure, just go slow," she said to him.

He ran into the barn and made his way to the steep old ladder. He looked at it for a moment and then up at his mother. She could see the apprehension in his face and smiled gently down at him.

"I made it up here just fine," she said. "You can do it."

Logan looked at the ladder and clenched his jaw. Melissa smiled. His face had lost the chubbiness of his baby years and she could see the beginnings of a hard jawline much like her father's. Logan gripped the ladder rung in front of his face and made his way up. When he stepped onto the floor, he smiled at her proudly and started walking around.

"Is this poop all over the floor?" he asked her.

"Yes, I think we've got a critter problem in our barn," she answered.

"Maybe Daddy can help get rid of them," he said absently. "He's coming tomorrow, he could help you."

Melissa inhaled and made herself stay calm. She didn't need to take her pain out on her son, even though she had explained to him the nature of divorce and separate lives several times.

"Daddy won't want to hang around here, babe," she said finally. "I'll just call an exterminator. He'd be better at it than me or your daddy."

"This place is really cool, Mom," Logan said. "Can me and Ryan have a clubhouse up here?"

"I'm not sure what I'm going to do with it yet," she answered. "Ryan is a bit too young to be up here and I might want to get some farm animals."

"Farm animals?" Logan said, surprised.

"Maybe," she answered.

"You're nuts, Mom," Logan said, grinning.

"Hey," she said, grabbing him and mussing his hair. "We're farmers now, boy! We ain't city folk no more! We need animals and overalls and a big red tractor that we use to chase goats out into the fields!"

Logan giggled and wiggled out of her grip. They climbed down the ladder and exited the barn, Melissa closing the barn door behind them and latching it. She looked at her new house and smiled, walking beside her eldest son.

"Ryan says he misses our old house," Logan said.

Melissa had sold the house that she and Kyle had bought together. It was a beautiful house in a desirable neighborhood. There was a large back yard and the tree-lined streets made everything look simply Rockwellian, but when Kyle left and the divorce was official, she couldn't rid his presence from that home. The pantry that he'd built, the paint color that he'd picked out for the office, the baseboard that he'd installed in the bedroom—he was in all of it and she had to get away. Luckily, the house sold rather quickly, her day job was steady and reliable, and her second book did well with her niche audience. She was able to purchase a little under eight acres of land with the old barn (the farmhouse had been struck by lightning and had burned down) and have a small prefabricated house erected for her and her kids.

"We'll all get used to this just fine," she assured Logan. "Ryan is still just a little guy. He'll adjust faster than you and me put together."

They walked into the house, her arm draped over her oldest child's shoulder. She went upstairs to check on Ryan, her five-year-old son. He was sitting on his floor, surrounded by mountains of his toys and stuffed animals. He looked up at her and smiled innocently. She smiled back.

"Hi, Mommy!" he said to her happily.

"Hey, baby," she replied.

"Mommy? Can we get pizza order for dinner tonight?" Pizza order was his way of asking for Domino's Pizza. Melissa laughed.

"We live out in the country now, baby," she said to him. "We can't do pizza order anymore. But guess what?"

"What?" he asked, bright blue eyes wide and interested.

"Mommy got us all our own little dinner boxes that you can help me make in the microwave, okay?" Dinner boxes meant that they had kids-themed TV dinners while she got to suffer through a Lean Cuisine.

"Okay!" Ryan said, excited. He loved to help out in the kitchen, and pushing the buttons on the microwave was the best in his opinion. He returned to his toy mountain, forgetting about her, so Melissa made her way to her own bedroom to get it unpacked enough for her to sleep in that night.

After the boys had been put to bed and she was snuggled under her own familiar blankets in a new room, Melissa cried. Bitter tears streamed from her eyes and made her pillow soggy. She cried for everything that she had lost when Kyle left her. She cried for everything that her sons had lost when Kyle left them. She cried for the memories that she knew Logan would always have of her crying when she confronted Kyle about his infidelity. She cried knowing Ryan wouldn't remember what it was like to have a complete family. The pain eased out of her eventually and she remembered her therapy. She remembered to remind herself of how lucky she actually was. She could support herself and her kids with her day job, and Kyle faithfully paid child support. Her writing career was finally starting to become steady and promising, and that, coupled with the sale of her previous home and her day job, enabled her to afford her dream home in the country. Kyle used to share that dream with her, but she forced herself not to dwell on that. She was home. This was all hers and her boys'. Everything was going to be just fine, damn it. It had to be. It was her turn at something good.

Chapter Two

The next day she made waffles and bacon for breakfast. It was a favorite breakfast of the boys and Kyle had loved it, too. He was coming to get the boys soon and she briefly considered keeping a plate warm for him in the oven, but thought better of it. Even though her instinct was to be welcoming and hospitable, especially in her new home, his eating habits were no longer her concern.

"Mom," Logan began. "Will the Easter Bunny still come here even if we're at Daddy's?"

"Yes," Melissa answered. "Your daddy will give you your presents from him and then he'll bring you home nice and early tomorrow so you can see what the Easter Bunny left you."

"Will the Easter Bunny hide eggs for us to find?" Ryan asked.

"Maybe not this year. Since this place is new, he might want to get more familiar with it before he starts hiding stuff all over the place," she said, smiling to herself. She wasn't going to be able to do the Santa/Easter Bunny thing for much longer. The boys were growing up entirely too fast.

Kyle pulled up and knocked on the old-fashioned screen door. Pulling her robe tight around her, Melissa went to the door and unlatched the hook. Kyle opened the door himself and stepped inside. He looked around and inhaled deeply.

"Mmmm, I smell bacon," he said with a smile.

"Yeah, the boys are just finishing up," Melissa answered, turning away from him and walking back to the kitchen.

Dumb-Dumb, hearing Kyle's voice, came running into the entryway, his whole body wagging.

"Oh, hey, Kohaku!" Kyle said excitedly. Dumb-Dumb whined and groaned, happy to see Kyle. Kyle got down on the floor and gave the dog a good scratching before standing back up.

"Are they all packed and ready to go?" Kyle asked.

"Yeah, their bags are in their rooms. Let me go get them," Melissa said, changing direction and going up the front stairs.

When she came back into the kitchen with two small duffle bags that contained favorite stuffed animals and a change of clothes, Kyle was sitting at her kitchen table joking with the boys and eating bacon that he'd snatched from a plate. Dumb-Dumb had his head in Kyle's lap, hoping for a piece of the bacon. Melissa frowned and set the bags on the floor and took her normal seat, which was next to Kyle.

"Boys, if you're done eating, go brush your teeth," she said more brusquely than she meant to.

The boys put their plates in the sink and raced each other up the stairs making a huge ruckus. She stared into her coffee cup and tried to ignore Kyle. When the silence got to be too much, she looked up at him. He was leaning back in his chair; his blue eyes, eyes that Ryan had inherited from him, were scanning the room.

"You want some coffee?" Melissa asked him.

"Nah, I'm good," Kyle said lazily. "So, Liss, you just went ahead and bought our dream farm, huh?"

Melissa bristled.

"It's always been my dream," she said simply. "I got the chance to do it and I took it. This will be good for the boys."

"Yeah, lots of space out here," Kyle said. "The house is really nice, too."

"Thanks," she answered quickly.

"Care to give me a tour?" Kyle asked.

"Uhhh, okay," Melissa answered. "This is the kitchen. Through that door there? That's how you get to the front door. Through the front door is the outside. There, end of tour." She smirked at him.

Kyle smiled back at her amiably.

"Still an asshole," he said fondly.

"So how's apartment living in the big city treating you?" she asked, feeling more relaxed.

"Cramped. Loud," he said.

Melissa raised her eyebrows at him, inquisitively.

"I was used to having my own space to escape to, before," he said. "Now, we live in this little apartment that only has four rooms and she follows me everywhere and the traffic noise just never fucking stops."

"I can't believe you're complaining already," Melissa said, teasingly. "You usually stay pretty deep in your denial until stuff starts breaking off or falling on your head."

Kyle laughed.

"I'm not in denial per se, it's just new," he said.

"You've been there for a while now," Melissa said, frowning at him.

"She's just so different from you," he said.

Melissa sat her coffee mug down on the table a little too hard and glared at him.

"Wasn't that the point?" she asked.

Kyle shrugged. Luckily, the boys came bounding down the stairs then and piled onto their father, demanding to know what activities he had planned for them that day. Kyle had one boy under each arm and was waddling toward the front door. Melissa picked up their duffle bags and followed behind.

Kyle pushed out of the unlatched screen door and set the boys on their feet. Melissa hugged and kissed them both and handed them their bags. She saw Kyle looking around again.

"If you don't mind, they want to come back a little early tomorrow for their Easter baskets," she said, looking at her feet.

"Yeah, okay," Kyle said. "You going to be okay way out here all by yourself?" he asked, grinning at her.

"This is my home now, so I'd better be," she said, trying to sound lighthearted.

"Okay, well I'll see you tomorrow," Kyle said. "If you need anything, you can call or text me, okay?"

"Okay," Melissa said, trying not to frown at him. He was

acting much friendlier than usual.

True, they had decided to try to be friendly with each other for the boys, and for the most part they did it very well, but Kyle was never really that talkative or eager to help. The boys piled into their booster seats and buckled themselves in, and Kyle pulled away, waving at her from his rolled-down window. She shrugged and looked down at Dumb-Dumb who was sitting next to her, watching the car pull away.

After she had cleaned up the breakfast mess and dressed herself in old clothes to keep unpacking, through the screen door she heard a car coming up her long driveway. She made her way to the front porch and cocked her head at the old Subaru parking. A tiny old woman with a nearly shaved head got out of the driver's seat. She opened the back driver's-side door and pulled out a carrier, looked at Melissa standing on the porch and smiled.

"Hi there," the woman said. "I'm your closest neighbor out here in the hollow (she pronounced it 'holla')! I'm Ida Conklin. I heard you had young 'uns, so I made you some cookies!"

"Oh my gosh, thank you!" Melissa said, taking the carrier from the small woman.

"They're snickerdoodles," Ida said. "I didn't know if anybody here had any of them allergies, and hell, everybody loves a snickerdoodle."

Melissa laughed.

"The boys will be lucky if I leave any for them," she said as she pried open a corner of the carrier and breathed in the sweet smell.

"Just a little welcome to Threenechex Holla'," Ida said.

"Oh, I didn't know this hollow had a name," Melissa said. "I just thought it was Route Four."

"Everything's got a name, honey," Ida said, smiling politely. Melissa nodded.

"It's a weird name, though," Melissa said. "Is it from some other language? It doesn't sound Native American or anything. It sounds like breakfast cereal." Ida flicked an uncomfortable look at Melissa and scuffed a foot on the porch.

"It's just some dumb name. It probably sounds weird

because I'm an old mud-mouth an' my accent makes it sound that way," Ida said. Melissa frowned but decided not to pry.

"I'm Melissa Caan," she said, extending a hand to Ida. Ida shook it firmly and smiled warmly. "Would you like to come in? The place is an unholy mess, but I've got iced tea."

"I'd love to," Ida said.

Ida seated herself at Melissa's warm wood kitchen table and looked around in naked curiosity. Melissa poured two tall glasses of iced tea and sat across from Ida. Without meaning to, she looked a bit too long at Ida's shaved head. Ida saw this and laughed, running a thin and heavily veined hand over her head.

"I had me a case of breast cancer a few years ago," she began. "I lost the breasts, but I kept the haircut."

Melissa surprised herself by laughing. She quickly covered her mouth with her hand and felt herself turn red.

"Sorry," she said, sheepishly.

"What for?" Ida said, smiling. "I was crackin' a joke and you was good enough to get it. Nothin' to be sorry for. Life is short and the closer I get to the off-ramp, the more I think that I shouldn't be wastin' the little bit I've got left on stupid stuff like hair."

Melissa self-consciously touched her hair that she had colored and cut once a month. Ida smiled at her knowingly.

"You're young enough," she said. "But when the chemo made all my hair fall out, I'd been a widow for years and I just felt like I had one less thing to do when it was all gone. And you have to admit, I look damn good sportin' just a pointy noggin'!" Melissa laughed again, slightly aghast at Ida's frankness.

"So," Melissa said, hoping not to let a silence settle in, "how long have you lived in the hollow?"

"All my life," Ida answered, taking a long drink of her tea. "I was born in the house I live in now. When I got married, me and Chuck tried movin' closer to town, but I missed the holla' so we moved in with my parents and helped them out. Most everybody out here is lifers. You don't leave a place like this for long. We're all prodigal sons. We all come home."

"I was born about two hours away from here. My grandparents lived on a farm that had been in the family for a really long time and I used to stay with them as a kid. I've lived in a big city and I've lived in the suburbs, but I've always wanted the farm life for myself and my kids," Melissa said.

"We all come home," Ida said, reaching out and giving Melissa's hand a squeeze.

They talked about the weather for a bit as they finished their tea. When Ida's glass was drained, she stood.

"I thank ya for the tea, honey," she said. "I only wanted to introduce myself, make sure you ain't a stranger to me. You don't want that in a place like this. I'll let you get back to settin' your home to rights, but you can come visit me anytime. I'm always home and if I'm not, I won't be gone long."

"Thank you," Melissa said, leading the way to the front door. "I'll do that."

Ida drove off and Melissa spent the rest of her day unpacking, finishing at around seven o'clock. She took one last bag of garbage to the cans outside and made herself a bologna sandwich for dinner. When she was finished, she decided to break in the large bathtub in the bathroom. She lit candles, put on some soft music, and filled the tub with steaming hot water. Her body was tired and lowering herself into the water was the best feeling she'd had all day. She washed herself first, to get that out of the way, and then leaned back and put a wet washcloth over her eyes.

As she settled herself, one of her hands brushed a sensitive spot on her side. Feeling a rush of electricity through her body, she ran her hand over the spot again. It felt so good, she started letting her hands go all over her body, searching out the parts that elicited the most interesting reactions. Eventually, her hand made its way between her thighs. She arched her back as her hand began a familiar routine. One hand stroked up and down her stomach, grazing her breasts and nipples occasionally, as her other hand massaged the swollen center of herself. Her movements started getting faster and she could feel her heartbeat increasing. Her breathing was heavy and she moaned lightly.

The bathroom door that she had closed to keep the steam trapped crashed open and a freezing-cold breeze rushed into the room. Melissa sat up, startled, and she heard a man's booming voice scream all around her.

"WHORE!" the voice said.

Melissa put her hands over her ears. When the breeze stopped moving and there was no other noise aside from her music, she scrambled out of the tub, dripping water everywhere. She ran all through her house, trying to see if someone had come in. She checked the front door to ensure it was closed and locked. She checked the door in the kitchen and it, too, was secure.

Heart racing, and shaking from the scare, she went back to her bedroom and looked in her closets and under her bed. She ran back into her bathroom and stood in the middle of the room, still naked, looking around. When the door had crashed open, the metal door stop screwed into the baseboard had bent completely to the side. She knelt down and looked at it in horror and awe. She sat and leaned her back against the wall. She listened for any other noises, and when she heard nothing, she dressed herself in some soft pajamas and went to find Dumb-Dumb.

He was sprawled out on the area rug in the living room, fast asleep. He wasn't anything by way of a guard dog, but she was sure that if someone had been walking through her house, the dog would have at least followed them around trying to get pats on his stupid head.

"Hey, Dumb-Dumb," she said, startling him awake. The dog quickly came to attention, sitting back and looking at her expectantly, his tail thumping on the floor.

"You didn't happen to see a boogeyman come through here, did you?" she asked.

The dog started panting happily and seemed to smile at her. Melissa rolled her eyes and stalked to the kitchen. Dumb-Dumb followed her expectantly. She put out the two Easter baskets that she'd made for the boys and gave Dumb-Dumb a Milk-Bone. She nervously did another round of the house, checking the boys' rooms (closets and under beds), and when she was certain that there was no one in the house, she turned off all the lights and went to bed.

CHAPTER THREE

Kyle was earlier than she expected the next morning. Melissa had been sitting on the swing on the front porch drinking her coffee and thinking about the night before when she heard the SUV coming up the long driveway. It was only about 8:30 and it was an hour's drive from his apartment, so the boys must have had him up with the sun.

Dumb-Dumb, who had been sitting next to the swing, stood at attention next to her. The SUV stopped and Logan and Ryan burst from their father's car, yelling "hello" to their mother and running as hard as they could to the kitchen to see what the Easter Bunny had left them. After the boys had gone in, Kyle sauntered up to the porch and sat next to Melissa on the swing. He patted Dumb-Dumb on the head and started moving the swing.

Melissa turned and stared at Kyle, her face demanding answers. Kyle's eyes darted to the side and back to the front, looking at her but pretending he wasn't. Melissa loudly cleared her throat, demanding his attention. Kyle turned and looked at her innocently.

"What?" he asked, finally.

"What's up with you?" she asked him. "You've been much nicer than usual. And sitting next to me like this? You usually try to stay at least a yard away from me. What?"

Kyle tried his best to look confused, but fourteen years together had afforded Melissa an insight to him and his bullshit that made her immune to his subterfuge. He smiled at her and she cocked an eyebrow at him. This silent exchange was still going on when the boys came zooming onto the porch to show off their Easter treasures.

"You were always good at holidays," Kyle said, watching his sons.

Melissa didn't say anything. She was looking at her boys, her heart concentrating on beating for those two precious creatures and their exuberant smiles.

"Things aren't working out," Kyle said quietly.

She took an indifferent sip of her coffee and waited for him to elaborate.

"You're not going to rub it in?" he asked her.

"What's the point?" she countered. "We're divorced. You chose a life with her and I started over. We moved on. What is there to rub in?"

"Aren't you just dying to ask me if I feel like I made a mistake in leaving you for someone I couldn't stay with for even a year?"

"No," she said.

"Come on, Liss, I'm making it easy for you to gloat, here," he said.

"Therapy and learning to live without you just sort of took it out of me," she answered, dully.

Kyle exhaled in an exaggerated way and resumed the swinging. Melissa chanced a sideways glance at him and saw his downturned mouth and downcast gaze. It was an old trick, but she knew she was falling for it.

"Do you need to talk about it?" she asked, staring straight ahead.

"No, that's okay," Kyle said, a hint of pout in his voice.

"Kyle Caan, I am a mother to two small children and I'd like to think that by now I can tell when someone is trying to unload on me. You, sir, want to talk to me. So get going," she said, as she playfully swatted his thigh.

"Oh, okay, since you insist," Kyle said, turning his body to face her.

"You said it's not working out," Melissa began for him.

"I think she used me," he said. "She's been pushing for marriage and kids since before I even left you. I always sort of chalked that up to an old-fashioned sensibility, but her work visa runs out soon and she's getting really aggressive about it. Like, she will not talk about anything else. She told me the other day that she'll just go home and marry someone there and forget all about me."

"Well, if you knew she needed to get married to stay here, and she was talking about it when we were still together," Melissa said, frowning, "then why is *this* the thing that is making your relationship not work? I mean, you knew about this from the beginning. And also, if you love her, don't you want to be with her? She has to leave, Kyle. Are you going to go with her, or are you going to just let her go?"

"I don't know," he said, watching the boys playing in the front yard.

"How is that?" Melissa asked belligerently. "I mean, I want to help you here, Kyle, I do, but you gave up everything to be with this woman. You left your wife and kids to be with her, and now you're using her need to get married to stay in this country as an excuse to not be satisfied with her?"

"Okay, so maybe it's not just that. I haven't been happy with her for a long time. I thought things would be comfortable, like it was with you and me, but it's not. She's not somebody that I like living with," Kyle said, still watching the boys.

Melissa scoffed rudely and watched the boys, too, fuming.

"I'm sorry. It wasn't nice of me to want to talk to you about this," Kyle said, finally. "But we were friends for years before we started going out and I missed you. I miss talking to you and getting your input on things. I didn't really realize that you were important to me in so many ways until it was gone, and I can't seem to replace you. I've tried. Guy friends aren't the same. She's not the same. I fucked up, I know I did, but I miss you, Liss. I really do."

Melissa sat staring at Kyle. She imagined the look on her face wouldn't have been at all different if he were shedding his skin and growing horns.

"I'm sorry things are hard on you right now," she spat. The truth was, she didn't want to hear any of this. She had fantasized about a moment like this, not long after he left, but now it was anything but flattering. She had had to struggle to learn how to be alone after he left, but he was never alone. She had to struggle to answer the boys' questions because he was gone, while he got the pleasure of being the superhero that swooped in and took them away on magical weekends. She'd made it out the other end. She still had her difficult moments when confronted with something that reminded her too strongly of the life they had had together, but she had survived nonetheless.

"I want to ask you something," Kyle said, sitting up and facing her.

Melissa nodded curtly, not meeting his eyes.

"Would it be okay if I could call you occasionally? I really do miss talking to you. I miss someone who gets references to movies that I love, and I miss hearing how your new book is coming. I miss your friendship, Liss."

Melissa blinked at him.

"This isn't me asking you on a date or to help me cheat... again. This is me asking to be a part of your life again, as more than just Logan and Ryan's dad. Can we be friends again?" Kyle said, reaching out to take her hand.

"I doubt *she* would be comfortable with this," Melissa answered, pulling her hand away from his.

"Well how about I do some real thinking and make a decision about that relationship? If I get married to her, yeah, she's not going to want me close to you. But if I let her leave and let the relationship just die, I'd be single and us being friends wouldn't intimidate anybody," Kyle said.

Melissa was already shaking her head, getting ready to argue his "logic," when Kyle held a hand up slowly in front of her face. He smiled sweetly at her.

"Okay, I get it. I jumped the gun. I'll work things out on my end and then I'll try to wear you down again." He stood, bent down, and kissed her forehead. She frowned up at him, completely at a loss for words.

"Happy Easter, Liss. And I do love this farm." Kyle headed down the porch steps and gave his sons hugs before getting into his SUV and driving away. Melissa exhaled loudly and resumed sipping her now-cold coffee.

CHAPTER FOUR

The boys were off at school and Melissa was seated at her desk working. The boys had been nervous about their first day at a new school, and she felt sorry for the millionth time about removing them from their established life. After they bravely climbed onto the bus and blew kisses to her from the window, she walked back to the house, guilt weighing her down.

Her cell phone buzzed and she picked it up. Normally, there was no internet access in the back country, but she had paid the cable company to run a line specifically for her. She needed internet access, and while her cell phone provider didn't have much coverage in the hollow, her phone was connected via Wi-Fi.

It was a text from her agent, making sure she was making progress on her latest book. She had asked to extend a current deadline in order to move since the house had been finished ahead of schedule. Melissa smiled and texted back that she was indeed working and would be working faster if she weren't being bothered. Her agent messaged back an emoji of a face sticking its tongue out. Melissa smiled and set her phone down, then worked until the boys came home.

The boys munched on Ida's snickerdoodles as they sat at the kitchen table doing their homework. Melissa still hadn't had a chance for a major grocery shopping trip, so they were having mac and cheese for dinner.

"Hey," she said, and the boys lifted their heads to her. "You guys want to go meet the lady that made those cookies? I bet she has more at her house."

The boys nodded enthusiastically. Melissa theorized that the boys ought to be familiar with the closest neighbor in case of emergencies. They should know to go to Ida. That was how things were in the hollow, and she knew it.

After dinner, they piled into Melissa's old minivan and drove out onto the dirt road. Melissa knew the turnoff for the next driveway and took it. Ida's driveway was as long as her own, nearly a half a mile, and when they finally got to the house, Melissa smiled fondly. If you did an image search on Google for "old farmhouse," Ida's house would have certainly been one of the first ten results. It was a two-story home painted white with no shutters or embellishments on the front. The tin roof and the large covered porch made it look so much like her grandparents' home that she felt a small pain of missing them, though, in relation to her own lifetime, they'd been dead longer than they were alive.

Ida came out on the front porch, waving at them.

"Well hey!" she said happily, by way of greeting.

The boys stayed back with their mother, shyness showing on their faces. Melissa leaned down to them after smiling and waving at Ida.

"Boys," Melissa said, "this is Mrs. Conklin. She made those yummy cookies and she's our closest neighbor out here in the country."

"Hello, boys," Ida said.

"Hello, Mrs. Conklin," Logan said politely.

"Hi," Ryan said, uncertainly.

"So you liked my cookies, did you?" Ida asked them, mussing Ryan's hair.

"Yeah," the boys said in unison.

"Well I got more in the house! If it won't ruin your dinner, you can have some!" Ida said, looking at Melissa.

"They've already eaten dinner," Melissa said smiling. The boys both grinned enormously at Ida.

"Well come on in, then!" Ida said, taking their hands and leading them into the house.

Ida's home was obviously old, but it was also well cared for and clean. The inside of the house smelled like wood smoke, boiled cabbage, and cooked pork. It was a pleasant, warm, homey smell. Ida took the boys to the back of the house where the kitchen was and produced an old ceramic cookie jar that looked like Cookie Monster. The boys gingerly put their hands in and each took only one cookie, thanking her quietly.

"Oh no, no, I know you can eat more than that! Dig in!" Ida said, holding the cookie jar. This time the boys dug in with more gusto, grabbing as many cookies as their hands could hold. Ida laughed, the fine skin on her face crinkling around her mouth and eyes.

Ida led the boys to a screened-in back porch and showed them an old wooden crate that was filled with toys and bottles of bubbles.

"You two just make yourselves at home and have some fun, okay?" she said to them. The boys smiled brightly and thanked Ida again. Melissa laid a hand over her heart, proud of her sweet, polite children.

"Alright, girly, how about some iced tea?" Ida asked Melissa. "The boys will be fine out here. We can give them some privacy."

"Sure," Melissa said. "And thank you for being nice to my kids."

"Oh, I love kids," Ida said, getting two glasses from the cupboard. "I have two of my own, three grandchildren, and two great-grandchildren. Children keep me feeling young, and there's always something to laugh about with kids around."

"That's the truth," she said.

"Is their father still at work?" Ida asked.

"I'm divorced," Melissa said, proud of herself for not stiffening or sounding offended.

"Hell, who isn't these days," Ida said, lazily. "I sure am sorry for ya, though. Is he still a part of those boys' lives?"

Melissa grinned at Ida. She'd forgotten this open curiosity that bordered on fence-hanging that the older generations tended to have. It wasn't meant to be rude and Melissa knew not to take it as such.

"He's still a good dad," Melissa said. "He just wasn't much of a husband."

Ida gave a huffy, brash laugh and put a hand on Melissa's.

"Well what is it that you do, honey? Do you work in town?"

"Oh, I do medical transcriptions. That's my main job, but the one I love most is that I'm a writer," Melissa said.

"Oh really? Ain't you fancy!" Ida said. "I read a lot. I wonder if I've read anything you've written."

"Oh, I doubt it," Melissa said. "I write for a publisher who publishes only homosexual romance stories."

Ida blinked at her. She looked down at her lap, her thin, wrinkled mouth working, trying to form words. Melissa smiled, but waited with a touch of apprehension at what Ida might say. Finally, Melissa felt bad for surprising Ida so much and kept talking.

"The rights of the gay community mean a lot to me. My best friend from childhood is a transgender lesbian, and my older brother is gay. All of the bigoted rhetoric pains me because I know that it hurts them, so I write stories that I think would be romantic fantasies these people I adore might like," Melissa said, conversationally.

"You're a good person, honey," Ida said. "I'm a little scared to comment. My grandson, Jonathan, says I always say the wrong thing when it comes to the gays and the blacks. I don't hate nobody and I don't like that the government is such shits to them people, but Jonathan says I don't use the right words. I'm not PC, or whatever the word is."

"It can get sticky," Melissa said, smiling.

"You've got that right," Ida said, laughing. It was obvious she was relieved. "In my day, we just used different words. I never saw that they were hateful, but I guess they are. I don't mean to be a bigot, I'm not. I'm just not using the right words."

"It's okay," Melissa said. "As long as your heart is in the right place, we can work from there."

"You're sweet, honey," Ida said, taking a big drink of her iced tea. "I'm thinking about putting a nip in my drink. Would you like one?"

"Oh, no, that's okay," Melissa said. "I'm not much of a drinker."

Ida smiled, got up, then took a bottle of bourbon from under her kitchen sink and put a good slosh into her glass. She took another long drink and made an enthusiastic smacking noise with her lips.

"So, honey," Ida began, "what are your plans with the old Schaeffer farm?"

"Schaeffer?" Melissa asked. "That's so weird. The people I bought the land from were named Rhinehart, but I found this carving in the hayloft of the barn talking about someone named Schaeffer and an axe. It was a lot like the Lizzie Borden rhyme you'd recite while jumping rope."

"Jesus God, I'd forgotten about that!" Ida exclaimed. "I can't believe it's still there! Wow, Tommy carved it up there in the early Sixties!"

Melissa stared at Ida quizzically.

"Well, it's a long story," Ida said.

"If you've got lots of tea, I've got time." Melissa smiled.

"Oh, alright. But, you ain't squeamish or nothin', are ya?" Ida asked.

"No, not really," Melissa said, frowning.

"Well, alright. You'da heard about it eventually anyhow," Ida said. "The Rhineharts were the kin of Thomas Schaeffer's wife, Liddy. They took possession of the house after...well after the big mess that happened there. Thomas Schaeffer inherited the house from his mother. His father had died in a thrasher accident years before and his mother took to her bed after. She never really recovered and she just sort of dried up and died. Thomas was a good-looking young guy, a typical good ol' boy. He drank and raised hell, but when he first saw Liddy he swore he'd stick to the straight and narrow if she married him. Liddy was a pretty little thing and sweet to boot. She married Thomas and moved to his family farm with him. They were poor, as a lot of us out here tended to be back then, and still are for the most part, but then Thomas got a job out at Lockheed Martin, and things really got better for them. They burned down the little old rotten barn that was there and raised that big 'un that's there now. That was a big deal, the Schaeffer barn-raising. It was a big party and everybody in the holla' came out to help." Ida had raised her small hand up to her temple and had that familiar far-off look that people get when old memories pull at them.

"Well what was the mess that happened?" Melissa asked, causing Ida to blink and come back to the present.

"Aw, honey," Ida said, suddenly sounding tired. "It gets ugly. You sure you want to know?"

"You said I'd find out about it anyhow," Melissa said. "I'll get completely distracted by it and have to spend all of my time researching it. You could save me a lot of time by just telling me."

Ida took yet another long drink of her spiked tea, frowning at Melissa.

"Thomas Schaeffer done got an axe and buried it in his two kids' backs, he took a break and ate some bread then took that axe to Liddy's head," Ida said.

"YES! That's the carving in the hayloft!" Melissa said.

"My high school boyfriend, Tommy Anderson, carved that up there," Ida said. "And it all happened...except for the bread-eating stuff. Tommy was a bit of a numbskull and he couldn't think of a good rhyme."

"So Thomas Schaeffer killed his wife and two kids with an axe? What happened to Thomas?" Melissa asked, sitting up in the hard wooden kitchen chair.

"My daddy found 'em," Ida said, quietly. "Thomas had turned bad. He was mighty jealous of Liddy, scared she's always cheatin' on him. But she wadn't. Liddy was a good woman. But Thomas started drinking. A lot. Got fired from that nice job at Lockheed and he took to just sitting around and guzzlin' whiskey and beer while Liddy worked as a seamstress and did odd jobs." She took another drink.

"I was in love with their oldest boy, Dave. At least as much as an eight-year-old can be. We played together, me and my brother and the Schaeffer kids, Dave and Donna. Dave was ten and Donna was six when it happened. My daddy needed something from ol' Thomas. I don't remember what. But he was callin' up at their house and nobody was answering the phone, so Daddy, scared something had happened, drove out there. He came back after about ten minutes, white as a sheet, and he said to my mama, 'We got to call the law, honey. Thomas Schaeffer done got an axe and killed that family of his. He's over there out of his mind, screaming about I don't know what.' It scared my mama so bad that she rustled me and my brother to our rooms. What happened after that...still to this day I don't know why Daddy didn't call the law first."

Melissa, already leaning as forward as she could, made a "come on" gesture with her hand and Ida took another drink and cleared her throat.

"Daddy called the Rhineharts and told 'em to get down to the farm. Liddy had a very protective father and two younger brothers. They drove down to that farm, and when they saw what he done did to Liddy and them kids, they lost it." Ida paused.

"What happened?" Melissa asked.

"Those three men drug him out to that barn and took a thick machine chain and wrapped one end around Thomas's throat and flung it over the center beam. They took the other end and put it on the hitch of their truck and they hung ol' Thomas Schaeffer right then and there. By the time the law got out there, Thomas was hangin' from that beam and they had to deal with the Rhineharts out of their minds from what they had found in that house," Ida said.

"What happened to the Rhineharts?" Melissa asked.

"Once everybody got a good look at them kids and Liddy, it was pretty obvious that them killin' Thomas like that was an act of temporary insanity. None of 'em got no jail time and they took possession of the farm and left it empty until you came and bought it."

"It must have been an awful scene for the authorities to just let them go like that," Melissa said.

"It was awful," Ida said, nodding. "Liddy's head, well, there weren't nothin' left of it. He'd hit it so many times with that axe that it was just mush. And then him murdering two little kids like that... Back then most people thought what happened to Thomas was his just desserts."

"I wonder why the Rhineharts wanted that property left vacant. Or why they eventually decided to sell it," Melissa said.

"They were heartbroken. They loved Liddy and those boys and they couldn't bear someone else living at their murder scene. But the ones that knew Liddy and the boys started dyin' off, and then the house got struck by lightning and burned down. I figure them Rhineharts think the memories are mostly gone now. No harm in sellin' the place," Ida said.

Melissa sat biting her lip, thinking of that strange incident on Saturday night while the boys had been with Kyle.

"You can still see the gouges on that center beam in that barn where that chain dragged across the wood," Ida said. "But us country folk, not many of us live in places that don't have their share of bad memories. Both of my parents died in this very house, but it's just a house. And that's just a barn, you hear?"

Melissa nodded.

CHAPTER FIVE

She was sound asleep when Ryan came into her room and whispered in her ear.

"Mommy," his tiny voice said. "Mommy, someone with big boots is stomping around my room."

Melissa was instantly fully awake, and she sat up in bed and looked around while Ryan watched her stoically. He reached out and took her hand in his and gently pulled. Melissa stumbled out of bed and followed her young child to his bedroom. He got up into his bed as soon as they were in his room and Melissa closed the door behind her, hoping not to wake Logan. She tucked Ryan in and kissed his cheeks, nose, and forehead.

"Do you think maybe you had a dream and heard the boots in your sleep?" she asked him.

"No, it was in the room," Ryan said. "They were big and stompy!"

Melissa turned her head for a moment and listened. Her breath was shallow as she strained to hear even the tiniest creak. Although her mind was certainly on Thomas Schaeffer and what had happened to her in her bathroom, she honestly assumed that her small child had just heard settling noises in the new house.

But then she heard it. It was faint, and not in Ryan's room. Eyes wide and heart practically jumping out of her mouth, Melissa realized that the sound was coming from Logan's room. She kissed Ryan again and tried not to appear alarmed as she made her way to the bedroom next door. The door creaked as she opened it and the heavy-booted footsteps stopped. Logan, thankfully a heavy sleeper, was undisturbed. She crept into the room and stroked his sandy hair before kissing his temple. As she was standing back up, right in her ear someone whispered, "*Get away from my boy.*"

She even felt breath tickle her neck. She jumped and spun around, her feet getting tangled in a pile of toys on the floor. She fell hard, making a pained sound as she landed. Logan mumbled and his blinking blue eyes stared down at her.

"What are you doing down there, Mom?" he asked.

Melissa was still looking around the room in a panic, searching for whoever could have whispered to her.

"Mom?" Logan asked again.

"Ryan had a bad dream, and I just came in to check on you, too," she said. "I fell on your toys. You need to clean this room, Logan, it isn't safe having the floor this cluttered."

"Okay, okay," Logan said, snuggling back under his covers. "I'll do it later."

Knowing that that was code for "I'll do it when you finally get mad enough about it to threaten something I want," Melissa got up and went into the hallway. She rushed downstairs to her desk and booted up her computer.

"It's a new house," she kept saying over and over as she pulled up the search engine. She typed quickly, needing to backspace several times. She'd watched the shows on television and read the stories. Confirming hauntings was becoming a business, and Melissa was in need of a professional.

Her search brought up thousands of results, and as she scrolled down, she saw a website for paranormal investigators who were based in the town closest to the hollow. They were called the Eastern North American Paranormal Society (ENAPS). She clicked the link and winced at the dated website and the spinning pentagram at the top of the page. The background was black and the text was a bright green color. She looked through the pictures of previous investigations that the team had done. Deciding that she needed peace of mind—and not knowing if it was an exorcism or an exterminator that she needed—she clicked on the link that read:

Is the other side camping out in your home? Contact us for help!

"Oh, God," Melissa mumbled.

A new window popped up with an email box. Pausing to think, she tried to decide how to approach these people without sounding batty.

Hello,

My name is Melissa Caan. I have a very unusual thing going on in my home. The really odd part is that my house is new. I bought a farm, where the old farmhouse had burned down, and I had a new pre-fabricated house built. But now I am hearing voices. Doors are banging open, my kids are hearing footsteps. My neighbor told me a story tonight about the previous occupants and the husband killed his family, and then was killed by his in-laws. I'm so sorry if this is rambling, but I'm very nervous about these occurrences and my children are both quite young. Is my situation something that you can work on? Please get back to me.

Many thanks,

Melissa Caan

She hit the "Send" button and exhaled. Dumb-Dumb was sleeping next to her, having appeared not long after she sat down in her rolling chair. She reached down and patted him on his stupid head and went up to her own bed. She sincerely hoped she didn't have to wait too long to hear back from those people. She hated the vulnerable feeling that was starting to creep into her mind. She had lived alone with her boys for a while, and now her fresh start was being marred by strange occurrences that may or may not prove that she was a paranoid and weak person who needed someone to make her feel safe.

She was at her desk the next day, getting some work done, when a ding on her phone alerted her to a new email. She opened her email program and saw that it was from ENAPS.

Hi Melissa,

I am writing in response to the email you sent us last night. Your situation, although vague, does seem to merit some investigation. We *would be happy to come to your home and conduct a formal investigation. If you decide that you want that, let me know and I will send you another email detailing exactly what we do. The cost of an investigation would include research about your property (public records, etc.) as well as an overnight stay of our team in your home. We charge $350 for an investigation. We accept PayPal, credit and debit cards, and checks. No cash, please. Email me back with your decision and if you are ready we will immediately move forward. We understand the stress situations like these cause and we are eager to move things along quickly.*

Much luck,
Drema Farrell
ENAPS Investigator

Melissa immediately responded, stating that the price was fair and that she would love to move forward. Not even a half hour went by before Drema emailed her again. Melissa was impressed and she almost let herself become hopeful. She decided to pay their fee via PayPal so that it would be immediate. Drema stated that they needed her address, the names of the former occupants, if she knew them, and a date that they could schedule the overnight stay. Melissa thought it would be best to make it a Saturday night when the boys would be with their father so as not to alarm them…or Kyle.

The email back-and-forth went on for most of the day, and by the time the boys came home, it was decided that the investigators would do a preliminary daytime visit the next day and the overnight visit in two weeks.

She treated the boys to dinner out and finally did a big grocery shopping trip. It took much longer than she expected and the cashier at the grocery store looked horrified to see her overflowing cart pulling into his lane at 7:30 on a Tuesday night. After she arrived home and as she and the boys were grabbing bags from the back of the minivan, Dumb-Dumb, who had been outside while they were gone, came limping up to them, whining.

"Mom, what's the matter with Dumb-Dumb?" Logan asked, alarm plain in his voice.

"I'm not sure," Melissa said, kneeling to get a good look at the dog. His feet weren't cut or swollen, and he appeared fine. She started feeling along his front legs and when she got to his right shoulder, he whined again and nipped lightly at her hand, asking her not to touch there. Frowning, Melissa stood and looked down at the dog. His shoulder hurt, but how did it get hurt? Could he have fallen? Maybe he was out on the main road and got bumped by a car? She remembered that she had a tether for him in the barn and she started walking toward it. As she was opening the large door, Dumb-Dumb yipped shrilly and started whining again. Melissa spun and saw the dog watching her intently, his head lowered and his hackles raised, making him look almost threatening. Melissa put her hand back on the barn door and Dumb-Dumb growled at her. When she removed it, he stopped. She put her hand back and Dumb-Dumb growled again.

The boys had slowly backed away from the dog and were looking wide-eyed at their mother. Melissa started walking toward them and Dumb-Dumb sat back on his haunches, watching Melissa intently.

"What on earth is wrong with you, dog?" Melissa asked gently, kneeling before him. He wasn't looking at her anymore. He was watching the barn. Melissa grabbed one of his ears and stroked it. He licked his flews and whined, softly this time.

"Come on, guys, let's go in the house. I'll bring in the groceries, while you boys give Dumb-Dumb some treats and some love, okay?"

"Okay," the boys answered in unison. The boys ran up onto the porch calling for Dumb-Dumb. Melissa stood in front of the dog, her back to the barn. Dumb-Dumb ignored the boys and continued to stare at the barn. The hair on the back of Melissa's neck was standing up and she felt her knees start to shake. Out of nowhere, she was terrified, and the feeling fell on her like a boulder. Suddenly scared of having her back turned to that barn, she slowly turned around. There wasn't anything there, just a big red barn...but then there was. In a fraction of a heartbeat, a black shadow materialized. It had no real shape, no form. It was just a black blob in front of the barn door. Dumb-Dumb was growling. The dog stood and limped until he was standing in front of her. Nothing moved. There was no wind, and no bugs were making any noise. The only noise that she heard was the dog growling menacingly at the shadow in front of the barn. She looked over at the porch and saw her boys looking, not at the barn, but at her and Dumb-Dumb. When she turned her eyes back to the barn, the shadow was gone, as if it had never been there. Dumb-Dumb was still growling, but he let her grab his collar gently and start to lead him into the house.

She got the boys and the dog situated in the living room, then turned on the TV just to have some noise in the house. She tried not to sprint every time she carried an armload of bags into the house, but having her back turned to that barn frightened her so badly that she could hardly pull off a calm demeanor. Dumb-Dumb refused to wait in the living room with the boys while she kept going outside, and opted instead to sit just inside the doorway, watching diligently. When the last armload of bags was in the kitchen and the van was closed up and locked, Melissa shut and latched the screen door. Then she closed, locked, and bolted the heavy front door. Dumb-Dumb watched the whole thing. She patted him on the head and kneeled down to him again. He seemed calmer. She touched his shoulder where it hurt and he winced, but that was all.

"You wouldn't let that thing near me or the boys, would you?" she asked him. She looked into his face and he looked back steadily. She patted him tenderly and ruffled the skin around his neck.

"Thank you," she whispered, before kissing his muzzle. "You Dumb-Dumb," she finished affectionately. The dog licked her face and she backed away and wiped her face in disgust. "Not too friendly, you," she said, annoyed.

CHAPTER SIX

"Oh, damn," Melissa said. It was the next morning and she was looking out the screen door, seeing Ida's car pulling up to her house. She was expecting the ENAPS people any minute and she wasn't really ready to discuss her little troubles with the neighbor.

"Hey, honey!" Ida said as she waved to Melissa as soon as she was out of her old Subaru. "I had a coffee cake and no one to share it with!"

"Oh that's great!" Melissa said, unlatching the screen door and opening it for Ida. She poked her head outside and listened for oncoming cars before following Ida back to her kitchen.

"Hope you don't mind me stopping by," Ida said, seeing Melissa's fidgeting.

"Oh, no that's fine. Besides, you brought cake," Melissa said smiling.

"Is everything okay, honey?" Ida asked, eyeing her.

"Yeah," Melissa said, taking in a big breath and puffing out her cheeks. "Yeah, I'm just…errm…expecting some company."

"Oh, well hell, I'm sorry. I can scoot if you need me to, you just had to say so," Ida said.

"No," Melissa said, sounding bland but resolved. "No, I'd actually like to ask you to stay here for this," she said. "You might be a good interview."

"What on earth has you so squirrely, girl?" Ida asked.

"Why don't you sit down and I'll get us some coffee and plates," Melissa said. When they were both seated with steaming mugs of coffee sitting in front of them, Melissa rubbed a hand over her face and tried not to look Ida in the eye.

"I've lived here for almost a week, so I wasn't really ready to talk about it, but..." Melissa began. She could feel herself blushing, but thankfully Ida sat and quietly ate her coffee cake.

"Okay, well there's been some things happening. Things that are scaring me a little bit and instead of just living with them and wondering, I contacted some paranormal investigators to come have a look around. I'm expecting them any second."

Ida frowned at her and slowly swallowed the mouthful of cake that was making her finely lined cheeks puff out.

"Wait a minute," Ida said, pointing her fork at Melissa. "What kinds of things?"

"Noises. Voices. The dog was freaking out at something in the barn that wasn't an animal," Melissa responded.

"What was it?" Ida asked, still frowning.

"I don't know," Melissa said. "It was there and gone so fast all I can seem to remember was that it was just a black blobby shadow."

"Hells bells," Ida said. "And why do you want me here? What do you mean I'm a good interview?"

"They might want to know that story about Thomas Schaeffer and his family," Melissa said.

For a tense moment, Ida sat staring at Melissa.

"You don't strike me as someone who does nonsense just for attention," Ida said. "If you say they's some strange things going on, hell, I got to believe that." Ida reached out and squeezed Melissa's hand. "I'll help however I can."

Melissa smiled at Ida and they drank their coffee and ate their cake until they heard a vehicle approaching the house. The both got up and went to the screen door.

"What in the hell is that?" Ida asked. Melissa laughed out loud and gaped.

It was a standard cargo van, but it looked like a moving version of the horrible ENAPS website. It was painted black and the writing was in the same neon green. On the hood of the van was the familiar (and probably trademarked) phrase, *Who You*

Gonna Call? Melissa laughed again, this time harder. Ida looked at her quizzically.

"What in the hell *is that?*" Ida asked again.

"Those are the paranormal investigators," Melissa said, wiping at her eyes. "I swear if a Goth gets out of that van, I'm locking the door and pretending I'm not home."

"Are they supposed to look like such morons?" Ida asked.

"They do look like a cheap parody of themselves," Melissa observed, still chuckling. "But they have a long list of previous investigations, and the contact that I've had with one of them seemed very professional."

"Well," Ida began doubtfully, "we can at least talk to 'em, huh?"

"Yeah," Melissa said, going out onto the porch, still smiling.

To her great relief, the man driving the van got out first and he couldn't have looked more conventional. He was wearing khaki pants and a blue polo shirt. The passenger was a tiny, round woman in black pants and a bright yellow silk T-shirt. She had very long hair that was softly curled.

"Ms. Caan," the tiny woman said, extending her hand to Melissa as she came up the porch stairs. "I'm Drema Farrell and this is my associate Bill Howarth."

"Thank you so much for coming out," Melissa said, shaking Drema's hand and then Bill's. "This is my neighbor, Ida Conklin. She's the one who told me about the murders that happened on this property."

"Oh, very good," Drema said, shaking Ida's hand. "It will be very good to talk to someone who is familiar with some of the land's history."

"Yes, it is always such an honor to speak with people of your age and wisdom when doing historical research," Bill gushed at Ida. Ida frowned at Bill, but then smiled.

"Son, I don't need butterin' up. I'll answer your questions without havin' to have my ass kissed up one side and down the other."

Bill blushed and Melissa burst into laughter all over again.

"Please come in," Melissa said through her laughter, holding the door open for everybody.

"I have coffee and coffee cake if you would like any," Melissa said, indicating that she wanted Bill and Drema to sit on the big cozy couch in her living room.

"Oh, no thank you," Drema answered definitively. Bill shook his head in the negative and took out a notepad.

"Okay, well, I guess we can begin then," Melissa said, sitting on an armchair that was sibling to the one Ida was perched on. Dumb-Dumb stalked slowly into the room, his limp slightly better. Melissa had made a vet appointment for him for that afternoon. He sat down at Melissa's feet and Melissa saw that Drema and Bill both noted his presence with nods to each other.

"Alright then," Drema began. "In your email to us, Melissa, you talked briefly of the incidents you've endured in this house. How long have you lived here and could you please tell us exactly what has happened?"

Melissa nodded and gathered her thoughts.

"I bought this land about nine months ago. The house that had sat here before had been vacant for decades and it was struck by lightning and burned down a year before. I didn't want to wait too long to move, so I got a prefabricated house to put up. The thing that took the longest, if you can believe it, was getting a cable line run out here. Those builders for the house company really hustled." Melissa knew she was rambling, but Drema and Bill were nodding to her politely.

"The first incident happened on the second day I was here. My sons were out of the house for the night and I was in the bathroom taking a bath. Suddenly, the door crashed open and I heard a man's voice call me a whore. Now I can't be certain that the door was completely latched, but I ran all through this house and nobody was here and the dog was fast asleep. And the doorstop was completely bent in!"

"As many details as you can give us about these occurrences are helpful," Drema urged. Melissa blushed furiously and looked down at her lap. She chanced a glance over at Ida, who was watching her in concern. She almost chickened out. It was nobody's business what she was doing in that bathtub. It was prurient information, plain and simple. But, she considered again and thought of jealous spouses and insecure men.

"Well," Melissa choked out, wringing her hands. "It had been a long day of unpacking and I just wanted to soak and relax, but, well. I was all alone, you see…"

"My Lord, look at the state you've got this poor girl worked up in," Ida said, touching Melissa's shoulder.

"No, no, Ida," Melissa said, looking at Ida and smiling. "It's okay. It's a detail that might help, it's just… Oh God," she said, burying her face in her hands. "I was masturbating," she blurted.

She heard Ida gasp loudly before falling into a fit of cackling laughter that Melissa couldn't help but find contagious. Melissa peeked out of her hands at Ida and laughed even harder when she saw how red Ida's face was. She still couldn't bring herself to look at Drema and Bill just yet.

"Oh honey," Ida said trying to catch her breath. "You poor thing…" but she couldn't finish her thought because she was cackling again.

"It's a perfectly natural compulsion, Ms. Conklin," Drema said professionally.

Melissa looked up, wiping tears from her eyes and trying to catch her breath as well.

"Well I know that," Ida said tartly. "I ain't no puritan, girly. That just shocked the skin right off'a me." Ida turned to Melissa and smiled at her. "I didn't mean to laugh, honey. I hope I didn't embarrass you."

"Of course not," Melissa said, returning her smile. "The laughing helped ease some of the tension, actually."

"And can you tell us about the other incidents, please?" Drema said.

"Sure. Umm, the next one happened a couple of nights later. My little boy came into my room and told me that he heard big boots stomping in his room. He's only five, so I thought maybe he'd had a dream, so I took him back to bed and tucked him in, but then I heard the heavy boots, but the sound was coming from my seven-year-old's room. When I opened his bedroom door, the sound stopped. I went to check to see if he was still asleep and as I bent over him someone whispered 'get away from my boy' right in my ear. I mean *right in my damned ear*,"

Melissa said, gesturing to the side of her head. "I felt breath on my skin and everything. It scared the hell out of me."

"Good God," Ida said, her hand on her chest. "That would scare the hell out of me, too."

"Me too," Bill said, laughing nervously. Drema shot him a look and he put his head down and continued writing on his notepad.

"Any others?" Drema asked.

Melissa relayed the occurrence that involved Dumb-Dumb.

"Was this the first time that you actually saw an apparition? Up until then everything else was auditory?" Drema asked. Melissa nodded.

"Is his name really Dumb-Dumb?" Bill asked.

"It is now," Melissa said, smiling. She patted Dumb-Dumb's head.

"Why on earth would you name a dog Dumb-Dumb?" Bill asked, smiling.

"He was my ex-husband's dog and I got stuck with him. I wasn't thrilled with that situation. That and I really hated the name my ex-husband gave him." Ida and Bill laughed.

"He seems to be a very loyal and loved pet," Bill said.

"Yeah, he's wearing me down," Melissa said.

"Ms. Conklin," Drema said, turning to Ida. "What can you tell us about the murders that happened here?"

Ida told them the same story she had told Melissa a few nights before. Drema listened intently while Bill wrote furiously on his notepad, filling several pages.

"I know sometimes in back country places like this people are buried on their own property or there are family cemeteries on the property. Do you know if Liddy and the children were buried on the property?" Drema asked.

"No. The Rhineharts took them and buried them in a big cemetery in town," Ida answered. "There ain't no Schaeffer family plot on this land neither. I played here all the time and I was here a lot as a teenager. I'da seen it."

"Where is Thomas buried?" Drema asked.

"He was cremated by the Rhineharts and put in a mausoleum in the farthest corner of the same cemetery away from

Liddy and the kids," Ida said. "They didn't want him resting anywhere near them."

"Thomas had no family to take possession of his remains?" Bill asked.

"Nah," Ida answered. "Liddy and the kids was all the family he had."

Bill returned his notepad to his bag and clicked his pen closed. Drema looked at him and nodded.

"I think that's all we need for now," she said. "Ms. Caan, I'll be in touch. Ms. Conklin, would it be all right if I got your phone number in case I have follow-up questions?"

Ida recited her phone number to them and Bill put it in his cell phone. They all shook hands again and Ida and Melissa walked the investigators out to the porch. When the van had disappeared beyond the tree line, Ida chuckled and sat on the porch swing.

"They seemed very professional," she said. Melissa nodded. "Their van is really goddamned stupid, though."

CHAPTER SEVEN

As a sign of good faith that everything would turn out okay, Melissa started making big plans for her little farm. She found a farm that sold chickens and chicken coops. The old man that she talked to was very friendly and helpful. They would put the coop up for her and put chicken wire around it and bring the young chickens right to her. She didn't even need to leave the house. She got six chickens.

She also decided to get some rabbits. These were more along the line of pets, but she knew that rabbit poop would be good for compost and she planned on putting in a large garden and canning vegetables for the winter. Maybe the garden wouldn't be so big this first year, but she was thinking long-term.

That Friday when the boys got home from school, they were shocked to see a brand-new chicken coop complete with clucking chickens, and a rabbit hutch with three little round bunnies inside. Their explosive excitement warmed Melissa and made her remember that she had wanted this not only for herself but for her boys. They wanted to name all of the chickens and to name the rabbits after the three of them, so one rabbit inevitably got named Mom.

"Do you guys want to eat dinner here or do you want to wait and eat with your dad?" she asked them when they had settled down enough for her to change the subject away from the animals.

"I want mac and cheeeeeeese!" Ryan said excitedly.

"Me too!" Logan said.

"Well do you want me to make you some or do you want to eat with your dad?" she asked again.

"I'm hungry now," Logan said.

"Okay then," Melissa said and went into the house to put the water on to boil. The boys stayed outside with the animals. Dumb-Dumb was out there with them. The vet had said that he seemed to be bruised, but his limp was nothing serious. The vet had asked if her husband had maybe kicked the dog and Melissa felt the blood fall away from her face in an instant.

Just as she was dumping the pasta into the boiling water, she heard Dumb-Dumb yelp, followed by her children screaming. As she was bolting for the door, she heard the dog begin to scream and then abruptly stop. Melissa exploded through the screen door, meeting her crying children as they ran to her.

"Dumb-Dumb was bleeding!" Logan said to her through his tears.

"His skin broke!" Ryan said.

Melissa kissed and comforted her boys and made them go in the house as she made her way to Dumb-Dumb. She could see him lying on the ground beside the barn. He wasn't moving.

She gagged as she stood over him and saw what was left of poor Dumb-Dumb. His back had been split down the center and she saw blood and red chunks all over his black fur. He was dead, of course. He had tried to crawl away from whatever got him; she could see that by the way his legs were splayed.

She backed away from the bloody mess slowly, sparing a tear for that poor, sweet, stupid dog. She ran into the house and called Ida and asked her to come over. As she waited for Ida to show up, she finished making the mac and cheese for the boys. They sat at the table, their little noses red, and sniffled over their bowls of obnoxious yellow food.

"Babies," Melissa said gently to them. They looked up at her.

"I'm so sorry you had to see that," she said.

"Is Dumb-Dumb okay?" Ryan asked.

Melissa swallowed a lump.

"No, baby, he's not. Dumb-Dumb has died." The boys started sobbing again. She jumped up and gathered them both into her arms and they sat together on the kitchen floor together crying until Ida called out from the living room.

"Eat your dinner, babies," Melissa said, going to Ida. "You want to have your strength for when Daddy gets here, okay?" They nodded slowly at her and mindlessly jammed spoons piled high with food into their mouths.

"I'm so glad you're here," Melissa said to Ida as she pulled her back out onto the porch.

"What's happened, honey?" Ida said, alarmed at the tears streaking Melissa's face.

Seeing Ida's kind and warm face made Melissa start blubbering. Ida, although a good three inches shorter than Melissa, gathered Melissa into her arms and swayed her the way one sways and comforts a crying child.

"Something killed my dog!" Melissa blurted finally into Ida's shoulder. "My poor dog has been completely ripped open!"

Ida pulled away from Melissa and looked into her face.

"Show me," Ida said simply. Melissa held onto Ida's hand and led her to the side of the barn where Dumb-Dumb had breathed his last.

"Jiminy Christmas," Ida said. "I seen the work of coyotes and bobcats and even a bear or two, but this is too neat."

Melissa looked back down at Dumb-Dumb and saw that, yes, it was too neat to be an animal attack. He had been *split* open, not *torn* open. Gasping loudly, Melissa looked at Ida in alarm. Ida held a hand up.

"I know where your head just went with that and you hold on a second and let me think," she said, obviously off her own footing.

"An axe could do that," Melissa said.

"Do you have an axe?" Ida asked belligerently.

"No, I don't," Melissa said.

"Then how in the hell could an axe have killed this poor dog?" Ida asked, pointing down at Dumb-Dumb.

"Well who would have done it?" Melissa asked back, matching Ida's belligerence. "Me? My two small children? The boys said he just started bleeding! Ryan said his skin broke! Oh my God, Ida, what the hell?"

Ida exhaled slowly and Melissa noticed that the old woman's hands were shaking violently.

"I don't have the foggiest damn clue," Ida said at last.

"What am I gonna tell people?" Melissa said. "People who don't know what's going on are going to come to some conclusions that make me look like a deranged dog chopper!"

"You're not gonna tell nobody nothin'," Ida said firmly. "We're gonna bury this poor creature and we're gonna go on livin' like nothin' happened. You hear me? This doesn't need to be holla' business."

"I'll need to tell Kyle something," Melissa said. "He'll be here in about an hour to pick up the boys for the weekend. It was his dog at first and he's used to being greeted by him. And the boys are completely traumatized by this. They're going to talk."

"You tell him an animal got him. The boys are still young and can be convinced," Ida said.

"I don't want to lie to them like that," Melissa said. "I don't want to make them think they saw something they didn't."

"You want them rememberin' it how it really happened, then?" Ida asked, annoyed. Melissa paused and thought about that for a moment.

"No, I don't," she said, finally.

"Wild animals are an everyday fact of life about country livin'," Ida said. "A pet being mauled by somethin' bigger ain't unheard of."

Ida and Melissa found a spot behind the barn where the dirt was dark and loose and they were able to dig a big enough hole for Dumb-Dumb. Melissa wrapped him in the blanket that she would lay down in the back of the van when he went for rides, and the boys threw dandelions on his body after it had been lowered into the hole.

"I'll cover him," Ida said to Melissa. "You get those young'uns ready for their dad."

Knowing that Ida meant talking to them about Dumb-Dumb's cause of death, Melissa took both boys by the hand and led them back into the house. After their weekend bags had been packed and set by the door, she and the boys sat down in the living room.

"A wild animal got Dumb-Dumb," she said simply. "Wild animals are everywhere out here in the country and sometimes they come to where the people live looking for food."

"That's not what happened!" Logan said emphatically. "I was standing right next to him! There wasn't any other animals around! Ryan saw too, Mom! It wasn't another animal!"

"Listen to me," Melissa said, leaning forward and giving Logan a steady look. "That's what happened. Wild animals can be very fast and maybe it happened so fast that you just didn't see it. You know?"

"No," Logan said. "I was standing right there."

"Logan," Melissa said, feeling her patience start to run low. "There's no other explanation that we can tell other people, people like Daddy. Okay? It was a wild animal that got him and we're all very sad, but that's how it happened. Ryan? Okay?"

Ryan frowned for a minute, but then he nodded slowly. Melissa looked at Logan and he was frowning at her stubbornly.

"That's what you're going to tell people, Logan," Melissa said, her temper showing. She pointed a finger at Logan.

"Fine!" Logan said, crossing his arms over his chest.

Melissa didn't feel good about it, but it was safer this way. It was also chickenshit of her. Ryan might grow up with a false memory of a wild animal, but Logan knew better and would always remember what happened, but there was no helping it. When an unseen force splits your dog down the middle, the chickenshit way is the best way to keep the world together a bit longer.

CHAPTER EIGHT

Kyle had been legitimately shocked and sad about poor Dumb-Dumb. He gathered his sons up and packed them away in his SUV before coming back and hugging Melissa tight.

"I'm sorry you had to go through that alone," he said.

"I wasn't alone," Melissa said, pulling away, swallowing the urge to cry again. "Ida was with me and she helped."

Kyle looked at Ida. Ida was eyeing Kyle intensely.

"I guess neighbors can be more than useless out in these parts, huh?" Kyle said, smiling his most charming smile.

"We take care of each other out here," Ida said.

"It sure looks like it," Kyle said. He turned back to Melissa and kissed her forehead. Melissa frowned at him and he simply smiled and stroked her cheek before turning away and getting into his SUV and driving off. Melissa waved to the retreating vehicle and swallowed hard. Ida put an arm around her waist and started guiding her back into the house.

"Come on, honey. I think you could use a snifter tonight," Ida said.

"Snifter?" Melissa asked, confused.

Ida pulled a silver flask from her bag and winked at Melissa.

"My daddy said it was medicine. You could use a bit, I think," Ida said.

Melissa allowed Ida to park her in a kitchen chair as she got two small juice glasses and some ice. Ida poured a bit of amber liquid into each glass and handed one to Melissa. Melissa smelled it and winced. She almost never drank and when she did, it was usually wine. Ida clinked her glass against Melissa's and took a drink.

"Bit o' bourbon will cure what ails ya," she said. "Go on. The heat in your belly will calm those sobs I see trying to pop out of you. Ain't no use crying over that poor beast now, so let's drink to him."

Melissa nodded and took a tentative sip of the drink. Its dark sweetness hit her before the burn of alcohol warmed her throat all the way down to her stomach where it settled, curling around and sitting like a hot stone inside of her. She took another sip, and the heat was a little less intense going down. Another, and she smiled at Ida. Ida smiled back and patted Melissa's hand.

"When it gets to your head, you'll be all better for a while," Ida advised. "Have you had dinner yet?"

Melissa shook her head no, taking another sip of the liquid, telling herself that she might need to make a shopping trip so that she could keep a bottle of this under her kitchen sink like Ida did.

Ida made herself at home, going through the refrigerator, freezer and pantry. She ultimately decided to make a couple of big sandwiches. She set out a bag of potato chips and placed a sandwich in front of Melissa.

"If you drink, you eat," Ida said sternly, pointing to the sandwich. Melissa obediently began eating. It was turkey piled high with meat and lettuce and there was even a sliced tomato on it. Melissa smiled at Ida as she chewed.

"Good girl," Ida said, beginning on her own sandwich.

When the sandwiches had been eaten and Melissa had put the plates into the dishwasher, they sat together in silence, munching on potato chips and drinking their bourbon. Melissa was definitely feeling the effects of the alcohol and she was thankful for it.

"What did you think of Kyle?" Melissa asked Ida.

"He's cute. The boys sure look like him," Ida said.

Melissa regarded Ida for a moment.

"I think he wants to try to reconcile with me," Melissa said.

"How do you feel about that?" Ida asked carefully.

"I don't know," Melissa said. "You know, when we were together, it was a dream of ours to move out to the country and get a farm. I mean, it was always my dream, since I was a kid, and he sort of grabbed onto it and made it his dream too. When he first came here, out of nowhere he started being nostalgic about that."

"But didn't he leave you for that woman he's with now?" Ida asked. "Does he cheat on everybody?" Melissa could tell from her tone the contempt that Ida had for cheaters.

"Yeah, he did. At the time, he told me how she was everything that he needed. It completely devastated me because I knew things were strained between us, but I didn't know that he would look to replace me like that. And not only replace me, but find someone so unlike me. It seemed like he just overnight decided that he hated everything about me and he couldn't get away from me fast enough," Melissa said. She was happily surprised at how no tears fell while she was discussing the matter. There was still a sort of dull ache that she felt when she thought of how Kyle had detailed to her all of the things that were great about her replacement, but she wasn't in pieces about it anymore. She was healing.

"So why isn't this great relationship scratchin' all his itches no more?" Ida asked.

"I have no idea. He was seeing her behind my back for almost a year before he left me for her, and they've lived together for nearly a year now but he's saying she's pushing the issue of marriage," Melissa said.

"That ain't unreasonable," Ida said.

"I don't think so either, but Kyle seems to think that she used him to gain residency in this country. But I don't know. That's an awfully long con," Melissa said.

"She's an immigrant?" Ida asked. Melissa nodded.

"She came here as a student and then was able to get a work visa, I gather," Melissa said. "But now those are running out and he said he can't decide if he wants her to go back to her own country and never see her again or marry her. Seeing how he's suddenly all touchy feely with me, I think he's planning on sending her packing."

"So he hasn't been completely clear about his intentions just yet?" Ida asked.

"No, not yet, but he did warn me that he's going to make a decision about what to do with her and that he wants closer contact with me. He said he misses my friendship. I don't know if I believe that. Like I said, he acted like he hated me when he left me and that wasn't yesterday. You'd think I would have heard that complaint sooner," Melissa said.

Ida was nodding, chewing thoughtfully on a huge mouthful of potato chips.

"I don't really know that I mind being alone," Melissa said, blinking fast. She'd been boo-hooing for so long over being spurned that she hadn't stopped often enough lately to consider how much nicer her life was as a single woman.

"I miss things like having help with the boys on a daily basis, and I miss sex (Ida coughed and laughed at that), and I miss feeling like I can share the mundane details of my life with someone, but I don't know. I think I like being without a man in my life right now. Kyle was really high maintenance and he could be horribly selfish and mean sometimes. And laundry is easier without his huge clothes taking up space in my washing machine."

"So what's got you confused?" Ida asked. "You sound like you're doing just fine without him."

"I get confused when I try to consider what would be best for my boys," Melissa answered. "Kyle was a bad husband, and when he was hot and heavy with his other woman he was a shitty dad, but before and after all of that, he's a really good dad. I have to think if this would be better for them, having that male influence in their lives on a daily basis. I mean, Logan is seven now, and he's really going to need a man in his life in a couple of years."

"That's bullshit," Ida said, taking a drink. "You said Kyle is a good dad, and a good dad can answer questions about puberty and erections over the phone just as easily as in person," she said, shocking Melissa. "Don't assume you need to sacrifice your own peace of mind by getting back with him for the boys. Those boys are going to grow up and leave and then you might be stuck living with a decision that you made for them and they didn't even stick around for it."

Melissa regarded Ida again, looking at her shaved head and lightly tanned, wrinkled skin.

"Tell me what you really think," Melissa said, grinning at Ida. Ida, not getting the sarcasm, took a deep breath.

"I've known quite a few people like ol' Kyle," she began. "They only care about themselves and they treat the people in their lives like they're disposable. When their use is up, they turn into garbage that needs to be thrown out and they move on to the next disposable person. They use people and demand everything from those they're with, but they never give as good as they get. They take and leave. That's what they do." Ida stuffed another huge handful of chips into her mouth and chewed, frowning at the chip bag.

"If they love themselves so much over all people, why can't they just spare everybody the pain in the ass of knowing them and just be with themselves?" Ida asked. Melissa laughed.

"Good point," Melissa said.

"'Course, I can't tell you what to do," Ida said. "You make your decisions as you see fit."

A comfortable silence fell and Melissa drained her glass amid the sounds of Ida finishing the chips in the party-sized bag of chips that they'd just opened. When she went into town to buy bourbon, she was going to have to make sure to have a reserve stock of potato chips in case of an Ida visit.

"I've got a spare bedroom that I keep made up in case one of my family comes to stay with me," Ida said. "I wouldn't think less of ya if you was uncomfortable staying here alone."

"Thank you, but I'm going to try to tough it out. Depending on how tonight goes, I might take you up on it tomorrow though," Melissa said.

"Well I sure hope that ain't the case," Ida said, standing. "I'm going to head on back to the homestead then, honey. At my age, stayin' up late don't make for a good morning."

Like Kyle had done before he left that evening, Ida bent down and kissed Melissa on her forehead.

"You call me if you need anything, you hear?" Ida said.

Melissa nodded and stood. She walked Ida to the front door. When Ida was in her car, she honked once and was off through the thick wall of trees. Melissa hugged herself and closed and locked the doors. She watched funny movies by herself, trying not to think about how there was no mopey dog sitting at her feet.

That night, she was awakened by the boots stomping around. She could tell that the sound was coming from the boys' rooms. She pulled the quilt up over her head and tried to pretend that she wasn't hearing anything. Eventually, the sound went away. That was all that happened that night and Melissa ended up sleeping extremely well, considering the awful day she'd had.

CHAPTER NINE

The next day was completely uneventful. Melissa got a lot of work done and actually finished early. Her agent was very happy with her progress and she decided to reward herself with a trip into town and the liquor store. She'd never really explored a liquor store before. Usually, she went to the wine section, picked out a cheap brand, paid for it and left. This time, however, she took her time. She was a little overwhelmed by all of the different mixers, liquors, liqueurs, and flavors. She left the store with a bottle of what the sales clerk had assured her was a very good Kentucky bourbon.

She then went to the grocery store and bought four party-sized bags of potato chips. She'd drop one off at Ida's house on her way back home. She also got a small rotisserie chicken from the deli section and a tub of coleslaw. She was on her own for dinner and intended to spend the rest of her evening on her couch watching bad TV.

Ida wasn't home, so Melissa left the giant bag of potato chips on an old wooden rocking chair on the porch with a note written on a napkin from the car. When she parked in front of her own house, she unloaded the van very much cognizant of a quiet terror mounting within her. The back of her head was prickling and tingling, and she knew that if her hair were shorter, it would be standing on end. Melissa fought the urge to turn and look at the barn for as long as she could, but eventually, she couldn't stop herself. She closed her eyes as she turned and stood for a long moment, her body facing the barn, but her eyes shut tight. Getting angry with herself, she snapped her eyes open and screamed when she saw the shadow. It was more defined. There were no legs. It was floating and it was coming toward her. It was a tall man with an axe slung over his left shoulder.

"Been out whoring around?" the shadow boomed at her.

Melissa dropped the bags she was holding and ran as hard and fast as she could to the house. Without thinking about the futility of the action, she locked and bolted the heavy front door and leaned on it, breathing fast and holding onto her chest, feeling her heart doing its best to make a dramatic escape.

The door thumped and shook violently against her back and she screamed and scrambled away from it. As she stood staring at the door, Melissa felt herself being grabbed around the waist from behind and thrown hard onto the floor.

"You filthy, cheating whore!" a voice screamed at her.

The sensation of being kicked in the stomach by a heavy boot knocked the breath out of her as she cowered on the floor. She curled into a ball and tried to get around the pain enough to remember to breathe.

"Don't you know I love you?" the voice whispered into her ear.

Melissa began to sob. She stayed curled up on the floor and covered her face with her forearms and cried. When all had been quiet for a few minutes, she uncurled herself and tried to stand up. She could only manage a deep slouch, the pain in her middle keeping her from standing straight. She looked around her and saw that nothing seemed to be out of place. She walked slowly to her front door, opened it, and walked out to the gravel driveway and collected the grocery bags. As she walked back up onto the porch, she caught a glimpse of the heavy front door as it stood ajar. There was an enormous black boot print right in the middle of it.

Still crying, she carried her bags into the kitchen and retrieved her cell phone from her purse. She took a picture of the boot on the door and emailed the picture to ENAPS with a description of the attack and of what had happened to Dumb-Dumb. She was plating some chicken and coleslaw when her phone rang.

"Melissa, this is Drema from ENAPS. I just got your email. Are you okay? Do you need someone to drive you to the hospital?" the voice over the phone blurted.

"No, I'm not hurt badly enough to go to the hospital," Melissa said. "I might have a bruise or two but I'm definitely doing better."

"Tell me one thing, Melissa," Drema said. "Was the shadow by the barn more detailed this time, or was it still shapeless?"

"It looked like half of a floating man holding an axe," Melissa said.

"Oh my God," Drema said. "It's building."

"What?" Melissa asked.

"Your presence is causing this entity to become emboldened and strong. It killed your dog, it physically attacked you. I'm not sure that your house is safe to inhabit anymore, Melissa," Drema said.

"I am *not* leaving my home," Melissa said, angry. "I have you to help me and I only have to wait another week for you to come for your overnight stay."

"Melissa," Drema began. "The overnight stay is to verify on scientific equipment that your house is haunted. You need to think about the safety of your children! Your dog was killed! You were physically attacked! Your children might be next!"

Melissa paused and thought on that for a moment. Imagining one of her children going through what had just happened to her made her guts twitch.

"I'm not leaving," Melissa repeated. "But I can have my boys stay with a friend until we can get this sorted out, okay?"

"That's very smart of you," Drema said, sounding relieved. "I wish I could convince you to leave as well, but I see that you're set. If anything else happens, call me anytime, day or night. I will talk to you this week and we'll be at your place on Friday." Drema paused. "Blessings on you, Melissa. I pray that you're kept safe from harm until we can bring help to you."

Melissa frowned and clicked the END button on her phone. She ate her chicken and coleslaw quietly at the kitchen table, a sullen mood dulling the taste of her food. When she had finished and cleaned up the dishes, she poured herself a bourbon and called Ida. She hoped that Ida was home and nearly started crying again when Ida answered the phone.

She explained what had happened and what Drema had said to her.

"So you think you can let the boys use that spare bedroom for a week?" Melissa asked.

"Of course," Ida said. "I've got a sofa bed for you too," she said.

"I'm not going to be bullied out of my home, Ida," Melissa said.

"I know you're settin' your jaw on this. I know you don't want to seem like you're abandoning your post, but you know, maybe in this case it might be better for you if you just stayed away until somebody can help you," Ida said gently.

"I hear you," Melissa said. "I do, but I really need this for myself. I need the boys to know that I didn't run and I need to be able to be here for anything. This house and this land have been a dream of mine for a long time and I'm not too keen on leaving after less than a month of living here."

"It ain't like that," Ida argued. "You'll be going back, honey. You're just staying away until it's safe to live there again. If that house caught fire, you couldn't live there until it got cleaned out and fixed up, you know. Think of it like that."

"I know you're saying this because you care, Ida, and I appreciate it so much and I appreciate you taking the boys so that I can sleep easy knowing they're okay. But like I said, I need to do this for me. I don't want to be the little woman all alone in the wilderness who tucks tail and runs whenever she gets scared," Melissa said.

"I could argue that 'til the sun explodes, but I see you're dug in. I think you're being a bit of a dumbass, but it's your decision. I'm happy to keep those boys. Don't you worry about them."

"Thank you, Ida," Melissa said, feeling tears in her eyes. "Thank you for not letting me feel alone."

"You're not alone, honey," Ida said. "Not out here, you ain't."

Kyle brought the boys home before lunch the next day. Usually, it was close to dinner time before the boys were dropped off by their father. Kyle was definitely trying to scoot his way back into her life.

"How many chickens and rabbits do you have?" Kyle asked her, sitting at her kitchen table and drinking iced tea.

"I've got six chickens, all hens, and three rabbits. The boys named the rabbits after all of us, so there's a Logan-Bunny, a Ryan-Bunny and a Mom-Bunny," Melissa answered.

"No Dad-Bunny, huh?" he asked, seeming sullen.

"Not in this house, nope," Melissa said quickly. Kyle glared at her for a moment.

"You'll need to get a rooster if you want those chickens to lay eggs, you know. I know a thing or two about chickens. I could help," Kyle said. Melissa smiled a big bright smile at Kyle.

"I actually don't need a rooster for the hens to lay eggs. The hens don't require a rooster at all and since their coop is fenced in, the protective purpose of a rooster is null. I have Google, so I can figure out just about anything," she said, happy to burst his smug bubble. Kyle just chuckled and shook his empty glass at her, indicating he wanted a refill. Melissa frowned at him and jerked her head towards the refrigerator. Sighing loudly, Kyle got up to refill his glass.

"Well, okay, I'm full of it a little," he said, sitting back down. "But I bet you could use some help around here. Man, just keeping up with the basic yard work is going to take you all weekend with the mowing and weed-eating. And if you plant flower gardens or a vegetable garden, you'll have to do a lot of weeding and pruning. You could call me and I'd be happy to come help."

"That's nice of you, Kyle," Melissa answered politely. "The boys and I can handle a lot by ourselves and if I really needed some help, I know I could call Ida. She's a tough old bird and her flower gardens are gorgeous. She could teach me a thing or two."

"You're just not going to let me in, are you?" Kyle asked.

"I don't know what you mean," she answered, a chill in her voice.

"I'm trying to reestablish something with you, Liss. I'm making an effort here!" he said, getting a little too loud for Melissa's liking. She kept quiet for a minute to make sure the boys hadn't heard the raised voice and when she was certain that they were outside still playing, she leveled a glare at Kyle.

"You've had no interest in reestablishing a goddamn thing with me for almost a year now. You barely spoke to me in that time. And now, I don't even know what the hell is going on in your private life, but it seems that things aren't as hunky-fucking-dory as you seemed to think they would be after you divorced me, so what is this? Trying out all your options? How many other women are you trying to reconnect with now? Or do you just miss having someone take care of you like I did? Maybe you miss being around your kids daily? Or is it that now that the farm is a reality in my life, you got a nice stinkin' mouthful of what you left me to have. Doesn't taste so good now, does it?" Melissa was gritting her teeth and trying as hard as she could to not get too angry, but she was failing miserably. Her therapy wasn't helping her so much now.

"I made a big mistake, okay? Does that help you feel better? Do you need me to apologize? I do! I'm so sorry. I was a self-ish idiot and I was only thinking of myself and it didn't work out with a fairy tale ending like I thought it would. I took for granted that I could trust you and not have to worry about you just wanting something from me, okay? I want back in your life. I want to get back together, but really, I'll settle for being friends. I just want my family back. I want you back. I want to tell you about my day and have you actually remember what it is I do for a living. I want to be able to tell you about the new movie coming out that has me excited and for you to share the excitement with me. I want to wake up on weekends to the smell of a big breakfast cooking and the boys running around and being loud, knowing I'm safe and secure and that you're downstairs cooking for me and making the coffee just the way I like it because you love me." Kyle said his little speech in a hurried way, his voice still loud. To the surprise of both of them, Melissa burst out laughing. When she looked into Kyle's royally miffed face, she doubled over and laughed harder. When she was finally able to gather herself, she looked at Kyle and smiled warmly at him. She reached out her hand and he took it.

"We're divorced, Kyle," she said simply.

"I know that, but divorced people can be friends. Divorced people even sometimes get remarried," Kyle said.

"I'll never remarry you, Kyle," Melissa said calmly. "I know what cruelty and selfishness you're capable of. I'd never feel secure and safe with you like you did me. I'd never, ever trust you." Kyle slowly pulled his hand away from hers and stared down into his lap. Melissa grinned at him smartly.

"I know all of your tricks, Kyle," she said to him. "My guilt button is no longer yours to push. I can talk about us becoming friends. I think it would be good for us and for the boys. Best friends, though? I just don't know, Kyle. I'm not sure that I'm ready to share that much of myself with you right now." Kyle looked up at her, nodding. She smiled at him and he returned her smile.

"I guess this is a small victory, then," he said finally.

"We were always good at being friends," she said to him. "This shouldn't be too painful for either of us."

"Yeah, I guess," he said, sulking a little. Melissa kicked him lightly under the table. Laughing, he stood up. Melissa walked him out to the porch and after he had hugged the boys one last time, he turned to her and opened his arms to her. She hesitated a moment, but eventually stepped into him and let him hug her. She hugged him back, but hesitantly.

"I thought you should know," he whispered into her ear, "she's going back to her family. She's packing as we speak." Melissa laughed lightly and pulled away.

"Goodbye, Kyle," she said and walked back into the house.

Chapter Ten

The boys were excited at the prospect of having what Melissa called a sleepaway party at Ida's house. She asked them to go upstairs and pack their favorite toys and load them into the back of the van as she folded some laundry and packed a week's worth of clothes for each of them. When the back of her van was completely full and the boys were settled in, she drove to Ida's house. Ida, having heard the approaching vehicle, was standing by the steps leading up to her front door waving and smiling.

"Well hey," Ida said, opening the van doors for the boys. "You guys comin' to sleep at my place for a while?"

"Mommy says we're having a party!" Ryan said excitedly.

"We sure are!" Ida said. "I've got a whole truckload of ice cream down in the chest freezer and it just occurred to me that you guys ain't met my goat, Sophie. Do you guys want to help me feed her?"

The boys could hardly contain their excitement and Ida smiled at Melissa as she took the boys by their hands and led them around the side of the house to the back.

"You go ahead and take their stuff into their room, honey," Ida called over her shoulder. "Up the stairs, first door on the left."

It took four trips up and down the narrow stairs in Ida's old house to get all of the boys' stuff into the room. The room itself was as clean and neat as a hotel room and it had a large full-sized bed that both boys could fit in. When they traveled they always shared a bed, so this would not be a problem.

Melissa spent the day at Ida's. She was relaxed and calm and Ida cracked jokes to the boys. They made a huge pot of spaghetti that the boys devoured as if they'd never see food again and Ida wowed them by proving her enormous ice cream stash was real. As the boys sat in the grass eating ice cream cones in the orange setting sun, Melissa and Ida were sipping bourbon on the back porch.

"Kyle made another grand overture to me today," Melissa said, chuckling into the clanking ice of her drink.

"Oh Lord," Ida said. "Might as well tell me about it."

Melissa recounted what Kyle had said to her and how the visit had ended. Ida scoffed loudly.

"I'd put money down that the guy doesn't know how to do his own damn laundry and he's tryin' to sweeten you up so you'll wash his drawers for him," Ida said. Melissa giggled.

"His girlfriend worked full time, so I doubt she did everything for him like I did," Melissa said. "It was still kind of embarrassing for him, don't ya think?"

"Hell," Ida said gruffly. "Asses don't realize it ain't comely to be an ass. It's all they know."

They sat in silence for a bit, watching the sky start to turn deeper shades of purple as the sun set. When the chill in the air was too much, Melissa called to the boys to come inside for a bath. After they finished grumbling, she led them inside. They took a nice bubble bath in the large, old, cast iron tub in Ida's one bathroom. When the boys were clean and smelling of blueberries, she wiped down the bathroom as best as she could. She put the boys in their cozy pajamas and snuggled between them in the bed as she read them a book. When the book was finished, she kissed and hugged them both and told them that she would be back in the morning to get them ready for school. She stayed around for another hour to be sure that nobody refused to sleep, and when all was quiet, she hugged Ida. Ida's lips were pursed and white and Melissa knew it was because Ida was straining to keep her objections about Melissa not staying with her to herself.

When she parked her van in front of her house, Melissa bit back her pride and sprinted from the van to the front door, unlocking it fast and turning on every light in the house. She made herself a cup of coffee and sank into her couch and read for a bit before showering and going to bed. Everything was quiet and uneventful.

For three days.

On Wednesday, they were all in Ida's kitchen. The boys were doing their homework and munching on cookies Ida had made them. Ida was positively giddy to have children around to spoil. Melissa was editing a manuscript, enjoying the soft sounds of pencil to paper and cookies being crunched.

"Mommy?" Ryan said to her.

"Hmm?" Melissa said, not looking up from her work.

"Can I go back to my old room and get my Thor hat?" Ryan asked. Melissa looked up at him and smiled at his sweet face.

"Finish your homework first and I'll drive you. But we've got to be in and out, okay?" Melissa said.

"Okay!" Ryan said brightly.

"You need anything from home, Logan?" Melissa asked. Logan just shook his head and kept concentrating on his homework. She reached out and mussed his hair and he jerked his head away, annoyed. She smiled and continued her work until Ryan announced that he was finished. After Melissa looked it over to make sure everything with his homework was as it should be (he was in Pre-Kindergarten, so his home-work consisted of pretty simple stuff), they headed down the road to what Melissa started calling The Farm. Ryan exploded from the van the moment he was unbuckled from his car seat and ran to see the chickens and the bunny family. Melissa urged him to run up to his room and grab his Thor hat. His little legs sprinted into the house and she heard him stomp-ing up the stairs. Melissa was by the door, waiting to hear his stomping resume as he came down the stairs. Instead she heard Ryan start to cry. Thinking he couldn't find his hat, she started making her way to his room. When he started scream-ing, she bolted to him.

He was lying on the floor on his back, holding his side and screaming, tears running from his eyes. Melissa knelt by him and took him into her arms.

"What, baby? What happened?" she asked, feeling herself start to shake.

"I hurt, Mommy!" Ryan said, sobbing.

"Where? Where do you hurt?" Melissa asked. He pointed at his side and she pulled up his shirt. She gasped and pulled him close to her again, hugging him fiercely. She grabbed Ryan's little Thor hat and ran out of the house with her son, locking the door behind her. She sat in the front seat of her van, holding Ryan and rocking him in her arms. When his tears subsided, she pushed his side gently to make sure nothing was broken. He grunted, of course. There was going to be a hell of a bruise. She looked over her baby's head at the front door, where the black boot print was still visible. The top half of the boot print looked exactly like the red mark on Ryan's side.

Melissa kissed Ryan's face and promised him a pizza for dinner and as much ice cream as he could eat after. She buckled him back into his car seat and drove back to Ida's house, trying to keep from breaking down in tears. Ida and Logan were waiting on the porch, laughing and rocking in rocking chairs. When Ida saw Melissa's face, all humor drained away.

"Hey, string bean," Ida said, addressing Logan. "Would you mind doing me a favor and going and picking some dandelions for Sophie? That old girl ain't been given flowers by a cute guy in an age." Logan dashed off of the porch and ran to do his task.

"You took an awful long time," Ida said cautiously. Melissa burst into tears. Ryan, confused and still shaken, started crying, too. Ida, looking alarmed, gently herded Melissa to a rocking chair where she sat down with Ryan on her lap.

"Tell me," Ida commanded. Melissa needed a moment to calm down enough to speak and instead raised Ryan's shirt to reveal the boot print on her son's side. Ida gasped and jerked to an upright stance. After a moment, she leaned down and kissed Ryan's round, wet cheek. She folded both Ryan and Melissa into a fierce hug.

"Don't you worry about nothin'," Ida said.

Melissa got Ryan calmed down and got into her car for

the forty-five minute trek into town to pick up a pizza. The ENAPS people would be coming to do their research in two days. Just two more days.

CHAPTER ELEVEN

Ryan's teacher called the next day asking to speak with Melissa when Ryan's class was excused. Being in Pre-Kindergarten, Ryan only attended class for half-day, but after that he went to a daycare until Logan's class let out and the boys were both put onto the same bus. Ryan's teacher had requested that Ryan be kept at school after class instead of going to daycare. Worried about the number of issues that could have come about, Melissa rushed to the school. When she opened the door to Ryan's class room, she was stopped in her tracks when she saw Kyle sitting on a chair, Ryan sitting on his lap.

"What are you doing here?" Melissa asked Kyle.

"I got a phone call to please show up," Kyle said. He was obviously in the dark as to the reason as well. This had to be bad.

Ryan's teacher, a sweet middle-aged woman named Ms. Carlisle, sat down behind a small, low table and gestured for Melissa to sit next to Kyle. Melissa obliged and kissed Ryan on his smiling cheek.

"I called you in today because I discovered something startling on Ryan today," Ms. Carlisle began. "Ryan, can you lift up your shirt for me, please, sweetie?"

Ryan did as he was bid and Melissa's heart sank at the sight of the black and blue bruise that had the imprint of a boot at the center of it. Kyle jerked and adjusted Ryan on his lap to get a better look. He turned and looked at Melissa, a hardness in his eyes.

"I know that you two do not cohabitate. I also know Logan, and I had always thought that these two boys were very well-adjusted children. If this were any other case, I would have called Child Protective Services immediately without consulting the parents at all. Now, I asked Ryan how he came to be so brutally bruised and he told me that the black man did this to him." Ms. Carlisle leveled her gaze on Melissa. "Are you seeing someone who might have hurt this little boy?"

Kyle shifted in his seat and glared at Melissa.

"You're seeing someone?" he asked. "I mean, not that I mind that, but I would have thought that I'd have heard about that."

"Not black like African American," Melissa said wearily. "Black like a shadow."

Kyle and Ms. Carlisle stared at her with absolutely no expressions on their faces. Ryan reached out and started playing with Melissa's hair, a sign that he was nervous.

"Does Mommy have a new boyfriend?" Kyle asked Ryan. "Is there a man that comes and stays at your house who did this to you? What's his name?"

"Mommy only talks to Ida," Ryan said. "The man doesn't talk a lot. He just stomps around at night and makes Mommy cry."

"Ms. Caan?" Ms. Carlisle said.

Melissa began sobbing.

"If I tell you the truth you're going to think I'm crazy and take my babies away from me!" Melissa said through her hands that were covering her face. "I can't lose my babies. They're all I've got."

"What the hell are you talking about?" Kyle asked.

"My house is haunted!" Melissa said.

After she'd recovered from the looks on their faces, she tried to condense all of the happenings in her new home to the silent pair of adults. Ryan would occasionally chime in.

"I'm expected to believe this nonsense?" Ms. Carlisle said. "I've seen a lot of child abuse, but I don't think that I've ever had a parent blame it on a ghost."

"I've known this woman for almost two decades," Kyle said, sounding offended. "She wouldn't lie about something like that, and she wouldn't let someone hurt her children."

Melissa looked at Kyle, shocked. He put his hand on her shoulder and squeezed gently.

"I know you, Liss. No matter what's gone on between us, I know you wouldn't do this. And you wouldn't cook up some hairbrained story about a violent ghost to cover up an abusive boyfriend."

"Thank you," she whispered to him.

"Well I'm not as convinced," Ms. Carlisle said gently. "My concern is for the children, not Ms. Caan's feelings. This child has been brutally kicked."

"I know he has, and I have the boys staying with my neighbor until I am able to find a resolution to this problem," Melissa said. "We were only there for a couple of minutes for him to get something from his room."

"Could your neighbor have done this to him?" Ms. Carlisle asked.

"No," Melissa said. "She's pushing seventy and she's a tiny thing. Her feet aren't anywhere near that big."

Kyle lifted Ryan's shirt again and scrutinized the bruise. Ms. Carlisle looked at the two of them, her lips pursed.

"I don't feel good about this," she said at last. "I don't feel good about letting you think that I'm buying your ridiculous story. I'm going to watch Ryan very closely and the next time I see something like this, I *will* call CPS. This is a promise."

Melissa nodded and started to rise.

"You can just save the threats, alright?" Kyle said. "These boys are perfectly safe with their mother."

"That's okay, Kyle. Ms. Carlisle. Thank you for watching out for my son," Melissa said. She was unbelievably tired and just wanted to go to the office and get Logan and take him home and curl up with the two boys and eat junk food all night long.

She walked out of the classroom, Kyle and Ryan behind her. Ryan reached up for her and she picked him up, kissing his cheek again and smelling his sweet smell.

"Well I've got the day off," Kyle began. "Want to pull Logan out early and go do something to get your mind off all of this shit?"

Melissa smiled. Kyle had his bad side, and boy it could be bad, but he also had a good side, and right now, she was thankful that it was in the forefront.

"What are you suggesting?" she asked.

"Movie and burgers?" Kyle asked.

"You know, Kyle, I think this whole friendship thing might work out," she said, clapping him on the shoulder. "Look, I'm a mess… Can you go to the office and get Logan? I'm going to go clean my face in the bathroom."

Kyle nodded. They met in the parking lot ten minutes later, both boys excited at the change in schedule and the unexpected visit from their father. One movie and a trip to a drive-thru burger joint later, and they were all sitting on Ida's front porch. The boys were eating ice cream and Melissa, Kyle and Ida were drinking iced tea and watching the boys. Melissa had told Ida about the confrontation with Ryan's teacher and Ida had hugged Melissa.

"That's good o' that teacher to be watchin' for stuff like that, but she doesn't need to be addin' to yer stress," Ida said.

"If the roles were reversed, I would think the ghost story was bullshit. I have no reason to be mad at Ms. Carlisle. She's doing her job," Melissa said. Ida had chewed on her lip, thinking that over. It was obvious that she was torn between the need to protect Melissa and the bald-faced reason behind Ms. Carlisle's position.

All three of them teamed up and bathed the boys and put them to bed. After covers were tucked under chins and smooth cheeks were kissed, Melissa decided it was time to end the hellish day. Ida clapped Kyle on the back and lauded him for his help with the boys and she hugged Melissa. Melissa gave Kyle a brief, uncomfortable hug by way of goodbye and got into her van and drove the four short miles back to her house.

She was surprised when Kyle's SUV pulled in behind her. She stood on the gravel of her driveway, frowning at him.

"You got any coffee?" he asked. Melissa nodded, knowing that he had a long drive back to his apartment. He'd been so nice and helpful that day that she was able to overlook her discomfort at being alone with him.

She unlocked her heavy front door and turned on the lights. Kyle sauntered in and started looking around. He went up to the china hutch in her living room and opened it, pulling out that chipped old mug.

"I can't remember," he said. "Was this your family's or mine?"

"Yours," Melissa said, heading to the kitchen to start a pot of coffee.

"How much Caan family stuff is peppered throughout this place anyway?" Kyle called to her. She looked around the kitchen and saw at least three things that had been entrusted to her by Kyle's parents.

"Oh, there's a little bit in every room, I guess," Melissa called back.

"You never stopped being a member of the family to my parents, you know," Kyle said, walking into the kitchen.

"Yeah, I know. They were always good to me," Melissa answered. Kyle's father had died before they had split up and his mother died not long after the separation.

"Hey, you want what Ida calls a 'snifter' in your coffee?" Melissa asked. She opened the cabinet under her kitchen sink to show Kyle her small selection and he started laughing.

"What the hell?" he said. "You don't drink!"

"Well, I'm not making a career out of it or anything, but I do enjoy a good cold glass of bourbon every now and then," Melissa said. Kyle indicated that alcohol-free coffee would suit him just fine and she closed the cabinet.

Kyle seated himself at her kitchen table and Melissa had to swallow her annoyance at how at-home he looked there. She set a steaming mug of coffee in front of him and placed the sugar and creamer in front of him. He smiled up at her.

"We're still so familiar in so many ways," he said, adding absurd amounts of sugar to his drink.

"And in so many others we're strangers," Melissa said, reveling in the warmth of her own mug. Kyle looked up at her, and she could tell that he was hiding his own annoyance. She stifled a smile and took a drink.

"Are you at all scared to be here alone?" Kyle asked her.

Melissa felt her defenses slam up like a thick brick wall.

"This is my home," she answered simply. "I'm always best in my own home."

"Yeah, I know that about you," Kyle said. "But aren't you nervous about something else happening to you?" Melissa eyed him over her coffee mug. He was making it a point to not look at her.

"I try not to think about it," she said, finally.

"You think those paranormal people will be able to clear whatever it is out?" Kyle asked.

"Yeah, they seem to be confident that they can help me," she said, knowing it was a half-lie.

"Well, you know, if you ever were worried about being here, you and the boys could come stay with me. Or I could come stay here. I can be helpful," Kyle said.

"I know," Melissa said, choosing tact over open hostility. "Thanks for the offer."

Kyle looked at her expectantly, but when he saw that she was done talking, he sighed and took a drink of his syrupy coffee. He was seated in the kitchen chair that faced the hall that led to the living room and Melissa was seated opposite him, viewing her kitchen sink and cabinets. She tried to relax in the quiet moment. She looked at Kyle and saw that he was frowning at something behind her. Melissa put her mug down and felt her spine go iron-rod straight. Chills started rippling down her body.

"Liss," Kyle said quietly.

"Just be quiet," she snapped.

"What is that?" he asked.

Too afraid to turn around while still seated, Melissa launched herself out of her chair and ran to the other side of the room. She stood facing her warmly lit hallway and in the center of it, about six feet away from where she was just seated, was the shadow man. He was getting more detailed. Now there were semblances of legs moving as the shadow approached her. Reflexively, she held her hands out in front of her, totally oblivious of what Kyle was doing.

"Thomas," she said to the shadow, hoping for a reaction. She didn't get one.

"Thomas!" she said again, forcefully. "Thomas, you stop right there, do you hear me? You stay back!" The shadow kept advancing on her. She started backing up, arms still held out before her. Kyle jumped out of his chair and ran from the room. She backed into the cabinets behind her.

"Please, just stop," she said to the shadow man. It stood within reaching distance of her. It stopped advancing and stood before her. Without the shadow moving, she felt a smack on the side of her face. Her head swung to the side and her ear and the skin of her cheek felt hot. She yelped and tried to scramble away from the shadow, but she felt her hair being tugged hard and her head was snapped back. Another smack on the side of her face. Another on the other side. She was screaming now.

"You brung another man into my house," a deep voice snarled at her.

She was let go and she fell to the floor. She started frantically crawling out of the kitchen. When she was in the hallway, she got onto her feet and dashed for the front door. Kyle was standing in her driveway staring at her.

"Holy shit, Liss, was that what you've been living with?" he said, his voice shaky.

Melissa, panting and close to tears, nodded and sat on the top step that led up to her porch. She'd been very specific about having a large, covered front porch and it was one of the things that she loved most about her farm house. Now she couldn't bear to sit with her back that close to the side of the house. Slowly and cautiously, Kyle came and sat on the wide stair next to her. He put an arm over her shoulder. Managing not to cry, she reached up and felt the heat coming off her face. Both sides smarted and her left ear was throbbing.

"Don't let the boys in there until you know for sure it's been cleared out," Kyle said. "My sons can't live here. You might need to sell this place, you know."

"I'll get it resolved," Melissa said, tiredly.

"Don't put my boys in danger out of pride, Liss," Kyle said, warning clear in his voice. "I'm not accusing you of anything and I know you'd never hurt those boys, but don't be stupid."

Too tired and shocked to fight, she just nodded silently,

staring out at the darkness of her property.

"Go stay with Ida, Liss," Kyle said, his tone softer.

"I'll be okay," she said.

Kyle sighed and stood up. He held a hand down to her and she took it. He pulled her up and looked down into her face. Kyle wasn't much taller than she was and it was something that she'd always liked about him. Kissing and hugging were easy to do because nobody was reaching or bending. She let Kyle pull her into a warm hug. She noticed that he didn't smell the way she remembered, and just like that she knew. That was it, she was really over him. She patted his shoulder politely and pulled away.

"Kyle," she began. "It's been a hell of a day, but I think we need to have a discussion, you and I." She sat back down and patted the place next to her invitingly. Kyle obliged.

"This fire is never going to get re-lit," she said. "You know, we had a really great thing once upon a time. We were the couple that other people gauged their relationships on, you know. 'Oh, they'll never make it like Melissa and Kyle' or 'Melissa and Kyle are the real deal.' Do you remember that?"

Kyle nodded, smiling fondly.

"But we lost it. We had a hold of a comet's tail and we let go. We'll never catch it again. I don't want to keep having this conversation and I don't want you to keep gently prodding me, hoping to change my mind. I loved being married. Maybe I'll do it again one day, but it won't be to you. It's done. It's gone. I like the idea of us being friends because you were right; we were always good at that. But as far as a romance goes, no way, pal. Okay?"

Kyle didn't make a move, didn't say anything. Melissa reached out and took his hand. They sat like that in silence, holding hands for a long time.

"I'd better get home," Kyle said, standing up.

"Are you okay?" Melissa asked. Kyle started laughing.

"I really should be asking you that question," he said. "Are *you* okay?"

"I will be, don't worry about me," she said.

"I heard what you said," Kyle said quietly. "And I'll try to remember that. Is it really so bad that I miss you?"

"I wanted you to say that to me for such a long time," she said quietly. "My ego needed to hear it so badly, but it never came and I had to live with the fact that you'd moved on and were happy with someone else. But now, I don't know. I'm not happy that things didn't work out. I'm sorry for that. I'm also not happy that you want to come back. And, you know what's weird? I didn't know that I felt that way until you opened the subject. When you were being distant, I guess my imagination made something else of what could be, but when you started trying to schmooze me, reality came to hit me upside the head and I knew that things between us were done. The book is closed." She smiled at Kyle but he didn't smile back.

"The store went out of business," she said, poking him in the arm. He gave her a tiny smile.

"The chef has gone home," she said, poking him harder. He laughed and swatted her hand away.

"Alright, alright. I get it," he said. "I'm gonna go home and pout for a while, but then I'll be okay. Now that we've got that all squared away, will you please call me if you need anything? Or if the boys need anything?"

"Of course," Melissa said, smiling up at him.

"Okay then. You'd better!" He shook his finger at her.

"I will!" she said.

He left without the courtly kiss on the forehead, and she sighed a sigh of relief. When she was alone out there with no light except what was filtering out of her front room windows, she felt her guts knot up inside of her. She had to go back in there. She stood and stared up at the generic, but nice-looking, house. She set her jaw and felt herself stomping up the step onto the porch.

"This is *my* goddamn house," she said as she opened the front door.

CHAPTER TWELVE

Melissa sat on a chair across from Drema and Bill that Friday evening. They both came loaded down with electrical equipment, laptops, and stuff she didn't recognize. They also came with files and notebooks of information. After they had set up cameras and sensors all over her house and out in the barn, they wanted to sit with Melissa and go over the fruits of their research. Melissa had kept Drema updated on the occurrences, so ENAPS knew about all of the occurrences so far.

"Let me first assure you that lots of places, especially places that have been inhabited for hundreds, maybe even thousands of years, all have bloody histories. Accidents happen. Murder happens. We can forget all too easily how violent and horrible life can actually be. And for all of that, not all of these places have violent ghosts prowling the premises. This case is special and I think this one is special because of you, Melissa," Drema was saying. "I'll get to that in a minute, but I want to talk about the murders that were committed here in 1954 by Thomas Schaeffer and later by the Rhinehart men." Drema took a file folder from Bill and opened it. Bill sat quietly next to Drema going through a startling amount of papers.

"Okay," Drema said. "We were able to see a lot of newspaper clippings on it as it was covered extensively in the local paper. We couldn't see the photographs, but the reports are graphic enough. Now Melissa, are you sure you want to hear all of this?"

"I've been kicked, hit, my dog was killed and my baby was kicked. I think I can handle hearing about something that happened six decades ago," Melissa said.

"Alright then," Drema said, all business and calm. "Thomas Schaeffer had become suspicious of his wife Liddy's fidelity and began drinking heavily. He was a mean drunk and was fired from his job at Lockheed Martin after he showed up to work still drunk. This exacerbated his alcoholism and he became physically abusive to his wife and children. Mrs. Conklin was able to tell us about boot-print bruises on his children that she witnessed, and Liddy apparently could be seen frequently with bruises on her face and around her neck. He was a brutish beast of a man."

Bill looked up from the papers in his lap and nodded at Melissa.

"Liddy started going to her pastor for counseling and Thomas started suspecting that an affair was going on. By all accounts, this was pure paranoia on Thomas's part." Drema cleared her throat. "The murders happened one night after their pastor, a man named Sean Marshall, had come to their home to eat dinner with the Schaeffers. Apparently Mr. Marshall was very forward in talking to Thomas about his drinking and violence and it set Thomas off. After the pastor left, it appears that Liddy and the children went to bed, because they were all wearing night-clothes when they were killed. The children were murdered first. David Schaeffer, ten years old and Donna Schaeffer, six years old. They were cleaved through their backs with an axe. Thomas hit them so hard that their chests were completely opened. That's right, that axe went right through their backs and exploded through their chests. It was apparently very gory." Drema paused and looked up at Melissa. Melissa swallowed hard and nodded, wanting Drema to continue and desperately *not* wanting to think about her boys in the place of the Schaeffer children.

"Liddy was killed last," Drema resumed. "By what I've been able to gather from the reports, Thomas was able to knock Liddy down and he hit her in the head with the axe no less than forty-four times. There wasn't much left of Liddy's head." Drema closed the file and stood up. "I want to continue telling you this out in the barn."

Melissa nodded and followed Drema and Bill out to her barn. She went out there as rarely as possible, but it was where she kept the feed and hay for her chickens and rabbits. She opened the large doors and gestured for them to go in before her. Drema walked in and stood in the middle of the large room and pointed up at the center beam.

"If you look really closely," Drema began, "you can see the gouges in the wood from where the chain was dragged across as Thomas was hanged. Now, Thomas's murder was not quick and painless. His neck was not broken; he was strangled by that thick and heavy chain, and the friction from the chain pulling him up split the skin of his throat open in many places. They estimated that it took several minutes for Thomas to actually die up there."

Melissa stared up at the beam. She'd seen the rough, ragged gouges before. She imagined a man hanging there by a chain and she started shivering. Usually, she wasn't a squeamish person about murders and horror, but standing just below the place where the spirit that had caused her so much terror had died was not only surreal but terrifying.

"Mrs. Conklin said that there was an inscription in your hayloft about all of it?" Bill asked. "She said she and her high school boyfriend used to come out here to, well, they used to have sex up there."

Melissa's eyebrows shot up. Well sure, it was the Sixties." Ida surely wasn't a virgin bride." She smiled, and gave the center beam another apprehensive glance before leading the way up the ladder to the hayloft. She opened the door to let in the dying evening sunlight and pointed out the carving to Drema and Bill. Drema gave it a glance and Bill began photographing it. He looked back at Drema with a confused look on his face.

"What is this about bread?" he asked.

"Oh, Ida told me that her boyfriend was trying to find something that rhymed. It's just a careless insertion to give it a 'Lizzie Borden got an axe' feel to it," Melissa answered. Bill chuckled and continued taking pictures. He then took out a large piece of paper and a piece of charcoal and did a rubbing of the carving.

"Gee, you guys are thorough," Melissa said.

"You want your money's worth, don't you?" Bill asked, smiling at her. Melissa smiled back and nodded.

They went back into Melissa's house after that and Drema began getting some equipment ready. Drema was walking around with a small meter and she was unplugging various small electronics and taking notes on a notepad. Melissa tried to stay out of the way so she called Ida's house and talked to the boys and told them that she wouldn't be able to tuck them in that night, but that their father was going to pick them up the next morning. She told them that she loved them and promised to keep Ida updated on everything before hanging up.

"Melissa," Drema called from the living room. Melissa walked into the now cable-strewn room and looked at Drema. "I have this weird hunch about something, but I need to prove it first. I want to follow you around with my electromagnetic field meter and my electronic voice recorder. Would that be alright?"

"Sure," Melissa answered. "Um, why? Is it to make sure that I'm not a disturbance?"

"No," Drema answered simply. "Let's you and I go out to the barn and see if we can get this entity to talk to us."

Melissa made a "well fine, Miss Snooty-Pants" face at the back of Drema's head as they walked out to the barn. They needed flashlights at this point and Melissa was trying her very best to remain calm and not think about all of the things that could happen in the barn.

The barn didn't have electricity—it was an update that was on Melissa's to-do list—so Melissa placed her flashlight on a plastic tub that she used to hold feed for her animals and pointed it toward where Drema was standing.

"Okay," Drema said. "I'm going to stand here with you and I'm going to ask questions. Typically, spirits aren't vocal like he is with you so we use these electronic voice recorders and we ask questions and play them back, and every now and then we'll hear disembodied voices intelligently answer our questions. This is a big indicator that what you have going on is a spirit haunting and not something else. Okay?" Melissa nodded and Drema seemed to brace herself. Melissa hadn't considered that the ENAPS people might be nervous about this investigation, but after all that Melissa had told them, they would be fools to not be a little nervous.

"Are you Thomas Schaeffer?" Drema asked. "Why are you terrorizing this woman and her children? Why are you so angry? Why are you still here? Did you kill the dog? Can you tell me how I can help you? Do you remember the Rhineharts? Do you remember Liddy and Dave and Donna? Do you remember what happened to you?" Drema gave a long pause after each question. Melissa watched expectantly, but when Drema put the voice recorder into a pouch she was carrying Melissa got confused.

"Are you not going to play it back?" Melissa asked.

"Oh, no, not right now. We're going to do a lot of voice recordings through the night and then we'll upload them to a computer and sit and listen. That with the audio from the cameras all over your house will give us hours and hours of video and audio to go through," Drema said. "Now you just walk around here like nothing's out of the ordinary and I'm going to follow you around with my EMF detector and see if my hunch is right."

"Will you tell me about the hunch after?" Melissa asked, walking around the large room. Drema didn't respond, so Melissa sighed loudly and continued to pace around while Drema followed her, making notes on a small pad of paper. After what seemed like fifteen minutes, Melissa spun around and faced Drema, startling her.

"How long is this going to take?" Melissa asked. Drema looked down at her pad of paper and nodded to herself.

"I think I've proved my hunch. Come on, let's go back to the house," Drema said.

They walked back to the house in silence and when they entered the living room, Melissa saw that Bill had set up a large workstation in her living room. All of her furniture had been moved against the walls and Bill had set up two large folding tables in the middle of the room. There were three large computer monitors, and each monitor was showing six different images from cameras all over her house. Some of the images were night-vision green and some were infrared vision and more colorful. Drema nodded at Bill when they walked in and Bill lifted one of the cups of his headphones from his ear and looked at Drema expectantly.

"I'm taking her into the kitchen, where the infrared is set up, and we're going to talk," Drema said. Bill nodded and turned back to the monitors.

When they were seated at Melissa's kitchen table, Drema placed three pictures in front of Melissa.

"This is the Schaeffer house that stood here until it burned down," Drema said, pointing to the black and white photo of the small white house. Melissa looked at it closely. It was smaller than her current house, but there was really nothing of note about it. It was extremely simple.

"This is Liddy, David and Donna," Drema said, pointing to the next picture. "Does anything about this picture stand out to you, Melissa?"

Melissa leaned down and scrutinized the picture. As Ida had said, Liddy was a pretty thing. Beautiful, actually. She had short, curly brown hair and large eyes. She was wearing overalls and a button-up shirt and hugging her two children, both of whom favored her looks. Melissa looked back up at Drema and shrugged.

"It's not a strong resemblance, but the coloring is similar between you and Liddy," Drema said. Drema looked back down at Liddy.

"Only slightly," Melissa said, frowning. "My hair is longer, she's thinner. I think that's reaching a bit," Melissa said. When Drema frowned down at her, she continued. "I mean, I don't want to tell you your job, but I really don't see a resemblance aside that we're both brunette women."

Drema picked up the picture and frowned again. She looked at Melissa and back at the picture several times.

"Maybe you're just not seeing what I'm seeing," Drema mumbled, putting the picture back down in front of Melissa. Melissa knew when someone didn't want to admit they were wrong, so she said nothing.

"This is Thomas Schaeffer," Drema said, pointing at the last photo.

Melissa leaned down and bit her lip. The handsome, smiling young man looking back at her was a murderer? He wore his hair extremely short and he was wearing a white T-shirt with the sleeves rolled up. He was posing next to a blue pickup truck, a lopsided and easygoing smile making his right eye crinkle.

"Not what you expect, is he?" Melissa said, a nervous smile on her face.

"If you always think the way a person looks will dictate how they act, you'll always be surprised," Drema said.

"Yeah," Melissa said. "I guess you're right."

"I am right, Melissa," Drema said. Melissa looked up into Drema's face and frowned.

"I've researched a lot of bad people and I've also known a lot of bad people. You see a lot of beautiful smiling pictures of people who go on to do horrible things. When you get to be my age, you'll see that it doesn't take much to make people go bad and you're almost always surprised by who goes darkside. The second you go thinking you know what's what, life has a good time proving you very, very wrong."

"Oh," Melissa said uncomfortably. "Well, okay."

"Now here's how we're going to spend the rest of the night," Drema said, going back to her usual business-self. "You do whatever you need to do. There are cameras all over, as you know, and we're here with you if something happens. You go to bed when you're tired, eat when you're hungry. I'm going to be going around the house from time to time to get EMF readings and voice recordings, but Bill will stay in your living room. We'll stay until you wake up tomorrow and then we'll leave and start going over footage and audio immediately. It takes about three days to go through everything and then we'll come back and talk with you about your options. I can tell you now, I've already been in contact with someone I think can help you, but I'll keep that under my hat until a little later. Just know, you have one of the worst cases I've ever even heard of, let alone worked on, and I am making you my first priority, okay?"

Melissa nodded, and kept her eyes down on the table.

"Thank you so much," Melissa said.

"You're not alone, Melissa," Drema said in her no-nonsense

tone. "Don't go thinking you are."

Melissa nodded again, fighting the urge to cry.

Melissa offered to make Drema and Bill some dinner and they accepted with many thanks. She made a simple tomato soup and served grilled cheese sandwiches with it. When all of the dishes were returned to the kitchen, she washed them and put them away. She stood in the kitchen looking self-consciously at the camera sitting on top of her refrigerator, wondering what to do. She felt a chill touch her left side and she rubbed her arm to warm it up and left the room.

She found Drema in the master bathroom taking notes. When Drema noticed her, her eyes got wide for a moment before she relaxed and went back to her notes. Melissa tried to hide a small smile. Drema was on high alert and doing her damnedest to look cool and professional, but Melissa had just scared the beans out of her.

"Will you tell me now about the hunch you kept talking about earlier?" Melissa asked her. Drema gestured for them to leave the room and they went out into Melissa's bedroom. Melissa sat on her bed and looked up at Drema.

"I think he follows you around," Drema said. "When he is in a more quiet form, meaning he's not banging on things or being violent, he's always with you. At least that's what I think. You see, Thomas was terribly in love with his wife. It made him a jealous monster, but he really did adore Liddy. He was terrified of losing her. Something about you has him convinced that you are Liddy and I believe he's following you, watching you, pining for you."

"I really hope that's not true," Melissa said, her mouth downturned into an unhappy grimace. "That's not only creepy, but considering what eventually became of Liddy, that's scary as hell."

"Yes it is," Drema said. "Our research tonight should be able to prove or disprove my theory and we'll let you know. And Melissa, if it turns out to be true, I'd like to ask you again to reconsider living here full-time until we are able to get help for you."

"If it turns out that he's following my every move like you

think, that might actually be the thing that chases me out of here for a while," Melissa said.

"Good," Drema said.

"Is that why you were making me pace around in the barn?" Melissa asked.

"Yes," Drema said.

"Was he following me?" Melissa asked quietly.

"I'm not going to give a report on bits and pieces, Melissa. Wait until we've viewed all of the evidence and can give you a comprehensive and complete report," Drema said. "There's no need to scare you if we don't need to," she finished in a softer tone.

Feeling numb, Melissa nodded and watched Drema turn and walk out of her bedroom. Melissa changed into some comfortable pajamas and read for a while, trying to ignore the sounds of people moving about her home and talking. Finally, in the wee hours, her exhaustion took hold of her and she fell into a fitful sleep.

CHAPTER THIRTEEN

The alarm buzzed at her at six a.m. and Melissa put on blue jeans and a T-shirt before making her way down to where Drema and Bill were. They had already packed away most of their equipment and had returned her living room furniture to its original positioning.

"Anybody want any coffee?" Melissa asked them.

"Oh, no thanks," Bill said to her, smiling tiredly. "I'm going to go home and get straight to bed for about five hours before I start going over all of this audio and video."

"Same, but thank you anyway," Drema said.

When the gaudy ENAPS van had disappeared beyond the trees that lined the road that led to her house, Melissa hastily drank a cup of coffee and brushed her teeth. She jumped into her minivan and drove to Ida's house, completely unconcerned with the early hour. Luckily, Ida was up and the two women sat at Ida's kitchen table eating toast, drinking coffee and discussing the ENAPS investigation.

"You didn't see a similarity between you and Liddy, huh?" Ida asked Melissa.

"We both have brown hair, that's about it," Melissa said. "Drema said I just wasn't seeing what she saw, but I just think she didn't want to admit she was reaching for some sort of tie that wasn't there."

"I hate to pick that tight-ass's side, honey, but I think you are being a little blind on this one," Ida said.

"We look nothing alike," Melissa said incredulously. Ida

frowned and seemed to be trying to find a way to explain herself.

"I guess if all ya did was glance at that picture, you'd only just see the pieces of Liddy. But it's deeper than just colors and skinny asses," Ida began. "There's something about the way you two look when you smile. The way that the smile goes all the way to your eyes. You both have smiles that could light up a room. There's something about the way you two look with your kids. It's not an instant connection between you two, but it is there."

Melissa was frowning at Ida and chewing her toast thoughtfully when Logan sleepily wobbled into the kitchen.

"Hi, Mom," Logan said, walking over to Melissa and resting his head on her shoulder. Melissa turned her head and kissed his soft hair.

"Hey, you. Did you sleep okay?" Melissa asked him. He nodded into her shoulder and yawned widely.

"Can I have some cereal?" Logan asked. Ida went to get up, but Melissa held a hand up to her and got Logan's cereal herself.

"You've been such an amazing help and rock through all of this, Ida," Melissa said as she returned to her seat. "Thank you so much."

"You think nothing of it," Ida said seriously. "I couldn't leave you without no help. Would rub against my grain. I ain't no saint or nothin' but I ain't about to leave a mother and her kids without no help neither."

"I appreciate it, though," Melissa said, watching Logan shovel the brightly colored, sugary cereal into his mouth.

Ida smiled at Melissa and then at Logan.

"Boy, you've got the appetite of a big ol' hog, you know that?" Ida asked Logan. Logan smiled up at Ida, his mouth still full of cereal, and he dribbled milk back into his bowl. Melissa rolled her eyes playfully and Ida chuckled.

Melissa left the table to see if Ryan was awake yet. He was snuggled under the soft, fluffy blankets on the bed, sound asleep. Melissa snuggled in behind him and breathed him in. He was warm and still soft, like a baby. He wriggled in her arms. He turned over and looked up at her.

"Hi, Mommy," he said heavily. "What are you doing here?"

"I'm cuddling my baby boy," Melissa said.

"Okay," Ryan said and promptly fell back asleep.

He eventually woke back up and wanted breakfast. After the boys had eaten and brushed their teeth, Melissa helped them get dressed. She winced every time she saw the huge bruise that still covered Ryan's side. It was starting to fade to muted greens and yellows around the edges, but the middle, where the blow had fallen, was still a horrible reddish purple.

She packed the boys' overnight bags and they were all seated at Ida's table playing Old Maid when there was a knock at the door. Knowing it was Kyle, Melissa offered to get it. Kyle smiled at her as she stepped aside to let him into the house.

"BOYS!" Kyle yelled into the house. The thunderous sound of two little boys running as hard as they could to jump into their father's arms filled Melissa's ears as she stood aside watching the spectacle with a smile on her face.

"What are we doing this weekend, Dad?" Logan asked. Kyle looked up at Melissa and stood up straight.

"Well today we're going to go watch a movie and then we'll go back to my place and order pizza and play video games!" Kyle said, pausing for the boys to yell their approval of the plan. "And then tomorrow," he continued, "I thought we could come out here and get Mommy and we could go play miniature golf and get some ice cream!" The boys screamed their excited approval again.

"It's your time with them, Kyle," Melissa said. She was starting to get annoyed at his sudden and constant attempts to reassert himself in her life.

"My time can include you now that I'm single again," Kyle said, his tone matching her annoyance. "Even if I wasn't single, there's no reason that you couldn't come play golf and get ice cream with us. I mean, you get weekdays when it's all busy and I get weekends when we have all day to have fun."

"If you weren't single, it would never occur to you to suggest that we do a together family thing," Melissa said.

"Maybe not, but it should, especially considering what you're going through right now," Kyle said. "Come on, this is a friendship thing. As your friend, I'm suggesting you come have fun with our kids. As your friend, I'm trying to help you get your mind off of bad things," Kyle said.

"That ain't a bad idea," Ida chimed in. "Don't let this thing eat ya up."

"Come on, Mom! We'll have fun!" Logan said. "And ICE CREAM!"

"This is blackmail," Melissa said, laughing.

"No it isn't," Kyle said, grinning at her. "This is you being paranoid and having a hard time accepting a kindness from someone who's been a shit to you in the past."

"Do you blame me?" Melissa said.

"Not at all!" Kyle said, gesturing grandly. "So what do you say?"

"I can meet you there," she said. "What time?"

"I'll text you," Kyle answered.

Kyle and the boys left not long after, and Melissa and Ida sat on Ida's front porch listening to the wild noises that come from living so far away from a heavily peopled world.

"He seems to be trying," Ida said. "It's good that he admits to being a shit, too." Melissa laughed.

"Yeah, he wasn't always that good at admitting to being anything less than either a wonderful person or a perpetual victim."

"Being friends with the man, as long as he keeps to the boundaries, could be a good thing for those boys but it could be good for you, too. He's a trusted person with those boys and I know how you need all the help you can get with little ones," Ida said. Melissa nodded.

"It's just hard to trust him," Melissa said.

"I know it is, honey," Ida said. "And some caution ain't gonna hurt in the beginning. Just don't let yourself stay frozen. You might want to think about letting another man close to you someday."

"I'm nowhere near even wanting to think about that," Melissa said, laughing. "What happened hurt, but I really don't mind being single."

"I was widowed at fifty-four," Ida said, sounding wistful. "I loved my husband very much. I went on a date with a man from my church one time, but it wadn't right. After Chucky went, I just never saw the need to fill his space. Men, they don't like empty holes. They're always fillin' 'em. Women are okay with a bit of unused space." Melissa laughed again.

"I'm okay with that philosophy," she said. Ida chuckled.

Melissa drove Ida into town so that they could both do some grocery shopping. They had a tiff in the checkout line when Ida took issue with Melissa insisting on paying since most of Ida's purchases were for the boys. Ida lost the argument when Melissa deftly swiped her debit card through the reader. She smiled smugly and Ida grumbled about Melissa being a prideful brat. To mend the fence, Melissa let Ida treat her to lunch.

After Melissa had helped Ida bring the groceries inside, she was about to excuse herself to go back to her own house.

"I'd really feel better if you stayed around here today," Ida said. "It's about time to start dinner and you can help me cook and then we can just chew the fat for a while." Ida hesitated. "I just hate the thought of you over there by yourself. I ain't too keen on waiting for a phone call asking me to take you to the hospital." Melissa stared at Ida and nodded. She had no plans for the day except to waste away in front of her television and pray that no supernatural forces decided to turn her head into brain pudding.

They made simple skillet hamburgers for dinner and chatted happily as they washed dishes together. They sat on the porch drinking bourbon and talking about their lives until the sun had set completely. It couldn't be put off any longer. Melissa had to go home. Ida reluctantly walked Melissa to her van and stood waving until Melissa was out of sight.

Melissa put her minivan in park and walked to the barn. The chickens and rabbits hadn't been fed that day and she assumed that a better-late-than-never approach would be appreciated. The bourbon was warming her face as she opened the large door. She had started keeping a flashlight right by the door and she reached for it and flipped it on, not taking time to look around. She headed right for the food bins when she started feeling that prickly sensation that she had learned meant that she was not alone.

"You're home late," a male voice said to her. It had that familiar cadence and a tone of barely restrained rage. She spun around and standing under the center beam was the black shadow. Although it lacked all definition, being monochromatic, it held the hard and definite lines of a man with a large axe slung over his shoulder. Melissa licked her lips nervously and thought about bolting for the door, getting back into her minivan and going back to Ida's.

"I was at the neighbor's," she answered.

"Cheating whore," the voice returned. "You lying, cheating whore. What kind of mother and wife goes around fucking everybody but her husband?"

Terror started to rise like a volcanic eruption within Melissa as she started taking slow steps towards the barn door, her flashlight aimed like a gun at the unmoving shadow.

"I'm home now," she said soothingly.

"And it's time to do your duty," the voice said.

In a movement either too fast for her eye to see or simply instantaneous, the shadow was before her. It was taller than Melissa by at least six inches and she looked up into the blackness that ought to have been a face.

"Please don't," she said helplessly.

Her head was whipped to the side from a slap to her left cheek. Before she could recover, she was thrown on the ground and her shoulders were pinned back. The shadow had dissipated but there was still a force holding her still. When she felt her T-shirt being ripped open down the front, she started screaming. Her blue jeans were ripped open, and the little metal button that had popped off was bouncing somewhere on the wooden barn floor.

"THOMAS," Melissa screamed. "STOP THIS NOW!"

"I get mine too, whore," the voice said into her ear.

"I will leave here Thomas, and I will never come back!"

The weight holding her down was instantly gone. There was no movement of air that would signal a being with a corporeal presence removing itself from her. It was just gone. She sat up and looked down at herself. It had all happened so fast, she marveled. Her T-shirt was completely destroyed and the button and zipper of her blue jeans had been completely ripped out of the fabric. She was covered in goosebumps. She sat with her back against a wall and curled her knees up into her chest and hugged herself. When her breathing had slowed and the soreness of the attack started settling deep into her muscles, she stood and took off the torn articles of clothing. She walked them out to her garbage can and placed them inside. She then fed the rabbits and chickens as originally planned and locked the barn door behind her. When she was inside her house with the front door closed behind her, she was almost amused to find that she was terrifically furious.

"This is MY house, do you hear me?" she yelled up at the ceiling. She regretted it a moment later when it occurred to her that Thomas might want to have another conversation with her. But when nothing happened, she went upstairs and drew a hot bath for herself. When she felt warmed through and her body was scrubbed clean she dressed in her softest pajamas and called Drema. It was late, but Melissa had a hunch that Drema would be awake. She was right.

"You're an idiot for staying there," Drema said after Melissa had told her what had happened.

"Are you listening to me?" Melissa said, not in the mood to hear an "I told you so!"

"Yes, I am," Drema said. "By threatening to leave him, I think we might have something usable. But listen to me, this keeps escalating. He appears more solid every time he shows himself to you; you get why that alarms me, right?"

"Yeah," Melissa said, feeling tired.

"I'm going to call you on Monday, Melissa, and I'm going to have some answers for you then. We're working on as little sleep as possible to get through all of this video because you need a resolution to this right now," Drema said.

"I really appreciate it, Drema," Melissa said.

"This will not continue much longer," Drema said and hung up. Melissa laughed and climbed into her bed.

CHAPTER FOURTEEN

The next day was Sunday and Melissa spent her morning enjoying some quiet. She made herself a mushroom omelet and enjoyed that and her coffee while seated in the yellow light of her kitchen. She opened all the windows and basked in the sweet warmth of the spring breeze wafting into the room. She sang loudly to herself as she went out to the barn to feed the critters, and when she was back inside her house with no incident, she laughed at her tension. Her shoulders were practically hugging her ears.

Kyle texted her at noon and told her to meet them at the miniature golf place at two o'clock. That was enough time for her to get herself dressed and make the long drive out of the hollow and back to civilization. When she pulled into the little park, she saw Kyle sitting at a picnic table with the boys. When the boys noticed her, they ran to her squealing and wrapping their arms around her waist.

They had a great time. Logan was the best of the four of them, with Ryan and Melissa tying for last place. Kyle looked amused and annoyed at Logan beating him. It was all familiar to Melissa, sort of like summer camp every year when she was a kid. It was the same thing every year and she knew the layout of all of the cabins and buildings, but there was a newness to it every summer that kept it exciting.

Since it was dinner time they went out for hotdogs and ice cream after. The boys were starting to show the fatigue that was typical of most Sundays. Kyle didn't enforce an early bedtime with the boys when they were with him, so they always went to bed early on Sundays to make up for it. Melissa was buckling them into their car seats and Kyle was standing behind her, watching with a smile on his face.

"Would it be terrible if I invited myself back with you all?" he asked her. "You think Ida would mind?"

Melissa turned at looked at him. She was trying to remember her manners and not automatically think that there was some ulterior motive behind Kyle's every move. His apartment was empty now and maybe he wasn't too fond of immersing himself in the solitary silence that settled into every tiny corner of life when the boys were away. She understood that and she smiled at Kyle.

"Ida loves company," she said to him. "Come on."

When they pulled into Ida's driveway, she came out onto her porch smiling and waving as always. When the boys were free of their restraints, they ran up to the porch and hugged Ida as they had their mother. Ida laughed with them and kissed them on the tops of their heads. Melissa smiled at the moment, thanking whoever was listening for her luck in meeting Ida.

Again, they worked together to get the boys bathed and ready for bed. After stories had been read and soft, fragrant hair had been kissed, the three adults seated themselves at Ida's kitchen table. Ida produced a deck of cards and a bottle of bourbon and raised her eyebrows at them questioningly.

"I love it," Melissa said in answer.

Two hours passed as they sipped their bourbon and played Rummy. They joked and laughed and enjoyed the comfort of being with other people. When Melissa saw Ida let out a long yawn, she smiled and announced her exit. Ida graciously nodded and Melissa and Kyle said their goodbyes. Melissa drove back to her place, knowing that Kyle had intended to follow her home. When they were out of their cars, she silently led Kyle into the living room. Not all of the furniture in this room was new. The couch was one that they had bought together and she watched as he threw himself down and settled into a corner in the exact way he always had.

"Aaaaah," Kyle said, stretching his legs out. "This couch is still so awesome."

"Yeah, I still like it," Melissa replied.

"I want you to tell me about what those paranormal researchers found out," he said to her seriously. "Come sit with me and fill me in."

Melissa hesitated and took a seat in a chair that faced the couch. She told him about the few things Drema had told her and that Drema was calling her the following day.

"I want to be here when they do the cleaning...thing...or whatever the hell they call it," Kyle said.

"Why?" Melissa asked, crinkling her nose at him.

"I care about how this turns out, you know," he said. "My kids will live here. You live here. I want to make sure you're not getting ripped off." Melissa felt her blood pressure start to rise.

"You want to be the big man here looking out for the helpless little woman's interests?" she asked, gritting her teeth. Kyle sat up, looking alarmed. He realized his gaffe a little too late.

"Aw shit," he said, smiling. "I didn't mean it that way, but it sure came out that way, didn't it?"

"Yes. It did," Melissa said flatly.

"Okay, I'm sorry about that," Kyle said looking genuinely contrite. "I want to be here, though. Just because I'm an interested party, okay? I won't ask any questions or try to act like your big protector, I promise."

"But, why?" Melissa asked again. Kyle sighed and looked down at his lap.

"Ryan's teacher called me again," he began. Melissa felt a heavy knot begin in her stomach.

"And?" she asked, gesturing with her hands for him to go on.

"Well, of course she didn't believe the story you gave her about that bruise on Ryan," he said. "She seems to think that you're hiding a lover and that he's abusing the boys. Now, I don't believe that, Liss, I don't. But, I mean, there are things that I'm curious about. Our boy has a giant bruise on his side. You're suddenly drinking when I've never known you to have anything other than the occasional glass of wine with holiday dinners," he said.

"Wh-what are you trying to say, Kyle?" Melissa said, her

pulse racing and her head completely unsure of whether to feel angry or hurt.

"I'm saying that I want to see what my sons are being exposed to," Kyle said seriously. "I'm entitled to that."

"You were here!" Melissa said, pointing at him. "You saw! You ran away and left me alone with it! You saw!"

"I did," Kyle said. "And I don't think that I imagined it or that you somehow put anything into my head. I saw it. I did. And I really commend you on keeping the boys away from this place and I see how you're still doing your part to be a present mother to them. But I still want to witness this. It's not a sick curiosity or anything, but it *is* out of concern for my sons."

"What, did you make a deal with Ryan's teacher or something? Like you're suddenly the responsible parent and I'm a bad mother?" Melissa could feel tears start to blur her vision. Hurt had beat anger in her head and she was smarting from it.

"I took up for you, Liss," Kyle said gently. "I know you're a good mother. You're in a weird situation and other people are wanting to get involved. My family is involved in this and I want to be here, that's all."

"Then why are you concerned about my drinking? Or my having a lover?" Melissa asked.

"It's out of character for you," Kyle said.

"The me that you knew," Melissa shot back. "I'm allowed to change. I'm allowed to pick up new interests. Ida introduced me to a good bourbon on the rocks. I can't believe I'm having to defend a solitary glass of whiskey every now and then. I don't get drunk, I don't even do it every day!"

"Okay, fine. Fair enough," Kyle said accommodatingly.

"And having a lover is out of character for me? How in the hell would you know, Kyle? You know nothing about that part of my life. It's sure as hell none of your business!" Melissa said, relief washing over her that anger was coming to the foreground.

"If someone is around my kids, I should know about it," Kyle shot back. Melissa held back her next comment about Kyle being all too eager to have the kids around his girlfriend immediately after he left. It was unfair and she didn't want to keep throwing things in his face. She exhaled loudly instead.

"Okay," she said. "I guess you're right about that. Well I promise you, there is no lover or boyfriend. I'm enjoying being single and getting comfortable with just living with myself, okay?"

"Okay," Kyle said, easing back into the couch cushions.

"Did you question the boys about that? Ask them if Mommy had a boyfriend?" Melissa asked, ready to get angry again.

"I thought about it," Kyle answered. "I really did. But I decided to ask you instead."

"Well," Melissa said, feeling herself deflate. "Thanks for that."

"Yup," Kyle said comfortably.

"Hell," Melissa said, frowning at Kyle. "It isn't going to hurt a thing for you to be here. I'll keep you updated on all of that, okay?" Kyle smile at her and for a moment she saw the guy that she had loved so intensely once. She smiled back sincerely.

"Thanks," he said, getting up.

"I guess I'll be in touch," Melissa said, walking him to the door.

"Yeah, I'd appreciate that," Kyle said, turning to her. "I'm still allowed to worry about you. I've been a bastard to you, I know, but I never stopped caring for you."

"Okay," Melissa said quietly after a short pause. "I can believe that."

"Good," Kyle said, smiling and walking out the front door. Melissa stood in the doorway and shook her head.

She could see the reason in Kyle's request, but he had made some points that worried her. Melissa had known the side of him that could be manipulative and conniving, and she was gnawing on the concern that he was working on her in those ways again and using the boys for his fuel. And yet, he was being more polite to her than he had ever been since the divorce. There was a vulnerability to him that was new and she was almost annoyed to find that she still felt protective of his well-being.

"I'm sure this is going to prove that I really *am* an idiot," she said to herself as she shut and locked her heavy front door.

It was late, but she wasn't quite ready for bed so she made

herself an enormous chicken sandwich loaded down with tomatoes, lettuce, and mayonnaise. She plopped herself on her sofa in a way that would have made Kyle's established lounging position impossible and turned on the television. She watched the tail end of a movie she'd seen a hundred times and when her stomach was full of the heavy comfort of the sandwich and her eyes felt heavy, she made her way up to bed. As she snuggled into her bed sheets and smiled that all of her pillows smelled of her shampoo and not the less pleasant smell of Kyle's scalp, she remembered to be thankful for an uneventful evening. She missed having the boys in the house with her, but it was nice to not have to suffer any of the terrifying invisible violences that were too quickly becoming routine in her life.

Chapter Fifteen

"Can you drive into town and have lunch with us?" Drema asked Melissa. Drema had called at nine a.m., surprising Melissa.

"Um, sure," Melissa replied.

"Just come to my house," Drema said. "ENAPS doesn't have an official headquarters, but my home is the unofficial office. It's where Bill and I do our work. I'll give you our report when you get here. Is Chinese food okay?"

"Oh, sure," Melissa said. "Anything is fine. Is noon okay?"

Drema said noon was fine and she gave Melissa her address. Melissa took out her cell phone, input the address into her GPS app and calculated how long the drive would be. She'd been up since 5:30 to get the boys up and ready for school, so she'd already gotten her coffee and morning internet browsing done by the time Drema had called. Her day job only asked that she finished her assigned tasks by certain deadlines, which she did well, so an extended lunch every so often was never an issue. She showered and got dressed, keeping it casual with blue jeans and a blouse.

She drove through the hollow with her windows down, marveling at how dark it could be even on a sunny day because of the thick tree cover. The breeze was cool and there was a smell of clean nothingness out in the country. Melissa had to admit that she was feeling very optimistic. Drema was not exactly a warm and cuddly type person, but she was professional and she had assured Melissa several times that her problem was a high priority. Melissa trusted that ENAPS would help her.

She was driving down a quiet street of small, older ranch style homes when her GPS indicated that she had arrived at her destination. She smiled as she pulled into a driveway behind the horrible ENAPS van. Bill was waiting for her on the front stoop of the tidy brick home.

"I hope you're ready for this," he said, looking worn.

"I guess I'd better be," Melissa said, apprehensively.

Bill smiled at her and ushered her into the house ahead of him. Melissa walked in and was stunned by the house. It was very old-fashioned. It had dark wood paneling lining the walls and the carpet was a heavy shag in avocado green. The front room was a tidy and cheaply furnished living room. There was no television. Melissa guessed that this was where ENAPS typically met with clients. Bill walked past her and indicated that she should follow him. They walked through the almost hilariously outdated kitchen complete with orange Formica countertops and green appliances. Melissa gawked, reminded of her grandmother's kitchen. Drema was in a back room that was a converted bedroom. It was surprisingly spacious and held tables full of electronics and binders full of papers. There were filing cabinets under the tables, and bookcases completely filled with books on one of the walls.

Drema stood and shook Melissa's hand, the very picture of professionalism. Melissa smiled tightly and sat in the chair that Drema gestured to. Drema and Bill sat opposite her and they both produced notepads on their laps.

"The food will be here soon. We had it delivered," Bill said apologetically.

"Oh, no worries," Melissa said. "I would have paid for at least my bit."

"Let it be on us," Bill said seriously. "You're about to have a lot dumped into your brain courtesy of us. The least we can do is feed you." He smiled at her.

"Oh, okay," Melissa said. She started to feel nervous.

"When we do investigations like this, we like to categorize what kind of phenomena are being exhibited. There are many times when what's going on is because of power lines nearby.

There are times when, quite simply, the clients are full of shit and have us recording the sounds of their furnace kicking on. Other times, we are able to record otherworldly voices, but they aren't responding to our questions in an intelligent way. There's movement, but it's more of an instance of repetition. We don't consider these things to be actual hauntings. Those things make up ninety-nine percent of all of our cases. However, every now and then we come across something that indicates an intelligent and lucid presence. What you have, Melissa, is an intelligent entity haunting you," Drema said. Melissa swallowed hard and nodded. Although she already knew that she was being haunted, she was secretly harboring a small fear that Drema and Bill would not be able to find any definitive "proof" of anything and would therefore be unable to help her.

"We've got a buttload of evidence to show you to prove it," Bill said.

"There is quite a bit, yes," Drema said. "But the first thing I want to show you Melissa, is a short video clip from an infrared video camera that we had put in your bedroom." Drema leaned forward and looked at Melissa hard. "Do you remember my theory? That he follows you?"

"Mm hmm," Melissa said, her eyes wide.

Drema turned and flipped on a monitor on one of the tables. She clicked a mouse a few times and a bright orange and dark purple video started playing. Melissa understood that what she was looking at was an infrared image of her asleep in her bed. She was a bright orangish-yellow color. She was on her side in the video. She turned over to lie on her back and the place where she had just been was a slowly darkening orange color because it was still warm. Suddenly, the space she had just vacated was blacked out and a thick line went across her stomach. Melissa frowned for a moment, studying the picture, trying to understand. When it hit her, she gasped.

"He got into bed with me?" she asked, horrified.

"That's an arm draped over you!" Bill exclaimed, pointing to the screen. "I've never seen anything like that before, and I thought I'd seen some crazy shit!"

"Oh my God," Melissa said, staring at the paused video.

"There's more to support my theory," Drema said. She turned back to the monitor and clicked the mouse a few more times. This time, it was a normal video being taken. It was set up in front of the stairs that led from the front room landing up to the hallway where all the bedrooms were located. A hall light at the top of the stairs illuminated all the way down. Melissa had been adamant about making sure that the stairs were never dark or shadowy. The video showed her walking up the stairs and as she got to the fourth step, a shadow completely blocked her out for a moment. Melissa gasped and jumped. It only lasted a second and then she was fully visible again, continuing her ascent in complete ignorance. Drema clicked the mouse a few more times and the screen again showed an infrared recording. Melissa was standing alone in her kitchen when she saw a black blob stroke her left arm. The Melissa on the screen rubbed at the spot.

"I remember that," Melissa said. "I got a cold chill on just my arm!"

"He follows you everywhere," Bill said. "We've got EMF readings and video that prove it. He completely ignored us and stayed with you."

"And since your children were also subject to attacks, we wonder if he followed them as well," Drema said.

"We won't test that, though," Bill said quickly.

"No, there's no need to," Drema said.

"We've got plenty to work with," Bill said.

Melissa sat and stared at them for a minute. Her heart was thumping hard and fast in her chest, dealing with the adrenaline rushing about her body. The doorbell rang and Bill jumped up and left the room.

"I'm sure that's the food," Drema said. She eyed Melissa. "Are you alright?"

Melissa nodded mutely.

"We'll eat while we listen to some of the audio. He's a talkative one," Drema said.

Bill came into the room with a large bag of food. Melissa wasn't interested in eating. Drema set up three folding TV trays and pushed them all together. Bill placed the food on the trays and handed the paper packets of chopsticks to Drema and Melissa. Melissa meekly took the Mei Fun and Bill and Drema chose their own boxes and began eating. Drema turned and started clicking her mouse again. She turned back around and resumed eating.

"...a spirit haunting and not something else. Okay?" Drema's voice came from the computer. Melissa jerked slightly but relaxed.

"Are you Thomas Schaeffer?" Drema asked. There was a pause and nothing.

"Why are you terrorizing this woman and her children?" Drema's voice demanded. Pause. Nothing.

"Why are you so angry?" Drema asked.

"Cheating whore," a male voice said. Melissa gasped. Drema turned and paused the audio.

"That is the clearest electronic voice phenomena, or EVP, we have ever captured," Bill said, his cheeks puffed out with food.

"Bill, please swallow before you speak. I'm wearing your lunch," Drema said.

"Sorry," Bill said, only it came out as "Shorry" with his mouth so stuffed with food.

Drema glared at him for a moment and then looked at Melissa.

"It *is* the clearest EVP we've ever captured. If it weren't so frightening, it would be amazing. There's a tremendous amount of energy with this entity," Drema said. She turned and started playing the session again.

"Why are you still here?" Drema's voice asked from the computer. Nothing.

"Did you kill the dog?"

"T'weren't mine," the male voice replied. Melissa was able to stifle her gasp this time.

"Can you tell me how I can help you?" Drema's voice asked. Nothing.

"Do you remember the Rhineharts?" Drema asked.

"Never liked me anyhow," the voice said, sounding like it was clenching teeth.

"Do you remember Liddy and Dave and Donna?"

Melissa sat up and waited for an answer, hoping for something. There was nothing.

"Do you remember what happened to you?" Nothing.

Melissa sat back into her chair and took a dainty bite of her Mei Fun. The most interesting questions (in her mind, at least) weren't answered.

"I took one other EVP session while you were sleeping, but it was all quiet," Drema said. "More often than not, we don't get any EVP evidence from our investigations. We get a lot of fuzz and sounds that sound like whispers. I've never in all my years doing this had an entity talk so clearly. Usually, when we do get an EVP, we have to enhance the audio so that it can be heard clearly. This is not enhanced."

"I fell over in my chair when I heard it! I really did, didn't I?" Bill said, poking Drema in the side. Drema looked at him in an exhausted way and nodded.

"You know what's so weird about that?" Melissa began. "I was standing right in the barn with you and I didn't hear anything except you asking those questions. There weren't any strange noises or voices then, but on the audio it sounds like someone is talking right into the recorder. But what makes it *really* weird is that I've talked to him. I've heard his voice with my own ears on more than one occasion. Why couldn't we hear him in the barn?"

"That's a really good question," Bill said, smiling at her. "You're really taking all of this well."

"Yeah, well that's me," Melissa said, self-consciously.

"These entities exert a tremendous amount of energy to appear in or manipulate this plane of existence. The one in your house is the most active one we have ever witnessed," Drema said. Bill was nodding enthusiastically, his cheeks stuffed again with food.

"Our field is not exactly something that has been properly scrutinized by the global science community, but my guess would be that it depends on his mood," Drema continued. "If I'm correct, the times that you've heard this entity speak, it's possibly felt threatened or agitated, correct?"

Melissa recalled the times it had actually spoken to her.

That time in the tub, the time in Logan's room, and then in the barn. Yes, it was agitated on all three occasions. She nodded weakly at the ENAPS duo, who were eating voraciously while studying her face.

"It's not so different from a living beast, like us," Bill said. "You've heard the stories of a mother lifting a car off of a child in a desperate moment. Maybe energy to these sprits isn't so different from the way endorphins and adrenaline affect us. Maybe this agitation could be like a static rub that creates power for the entity. Can't be sure, but the levels of agitation seem to be the deciding factor on how solid it's presence in this world is at the time."

Melissa nodded.

"Okay," she said after a contemplative moment. "What do we do about it then? I mean, can you say that you've proven that my home is haunted?"

"Oh, yes," Bill said, his eyes wide as he nodded as seriously as he could.

"Very much so," Drema agreed.

"Well I don't think showing him a video of himself getting into bed with me is going to do much to improve my situation," Melissa said. "What do you do once the investigation is over?"

"Usually, a cleansing is performed. We take it on a case by case basis. If the client is extremely religious, we appeal to a church whose minister is sympathetic to the work we do, and they do a prayer group. That's where there's a group of people, fairly large usually, and they bring white candles and they walk through the affected house singing hymns and praying. We've found that in the less severe cases, something like that helps to neutralize the energy. If the client is a little less sure about religion, we do a sage smudge where we walk through the house wafting sage smoke through the whole structure, down to the tightest corner and crawl space. Now, in a case like yours, and we've only worked maybe four of them in the twelve years we've been doing this, we need help. Bill and I are very much out of our league. Again, if the client tends to be very religious, we contact the minister who is sympathetic to us and he will do an exorcism on the house, using prayers and religious items. We have no reason to believe that this is an inferior method or that it doesn't work. The clients are always happy with the results and their lives become quite normal," Drema said.

"I get the feeling that a minister coming to my home is not what you have in mind for me," Melissa said.

"Not quite," Bill said.

"There is a local woman who we've worked with a couple of times on some of our trickier projects," Drema began. She hesitated and actually looked over at Bill.

"She's a witch," Bill said.

"She's a Wiccan," Drema said. Melissa blinked at them both.

"Uhh," Melissa said.

"Just hear us out," Bill said, putting a hand up indicating that she should halt her judgmental horses.

"She knows things that your average person doesn't," Drema said. "She's a font of esoteric lore. When we're stumped about what to do in a situation, we turn to her and she is always helpful."

"A witch?" Melissa said. Drema pursed her lips and Bill gave Melissa a look that was edging on annoyance.

"Your house is really scary, Melissa," Bill said, talking slowly. "The spirit haunting you is violent. Walking around your house praying and wafting smoke into the corners is probably not going to help you."

"We need special help," Drema said.

"But, a *witch*?" Melissa asked incredulously. "I mean, aren't all modern witches either old hippies or Goth weirdos?"

Drema and Bill both snickered.

"You want to meet her?" Drema said, still smiling at Melissa.

"What's the joke?" Melissa asked. "What am I not in on?"

"Karen isn't what you'd expect," Bill said. Drema had gotten up and was on her cell phone murmuring to somebody. When she resumed her seat, she nodded to Bill and continued eating.

"She'll be here shortly, I guess," Bill said, stuffing food into his mouth.

"Well, okay," Melissa said. "Since we have a moment, I have a question. You've mentioned before that you find it alarming that he becomes more solid and detailed the more he shows himself to me. Are you expecting something bad to happen?"

"You mean worse than what has already happened?" Drema asked seriously. Melissa nodded. "I find a lot of things about this spirit alarming. Did you notice that his vitriol was aimed more at you than at his murderers? His rage is still aimed at a woman, not a man. Think about it. The dog, you, and your son have been attacked. Bill has never even felt so much as a chill in your home. He prefers to bully women, children and pets. The cowardice of the living man has carried over to the spirit. My concern with his progressing clarity is that perhaps he might reenact that horrible night when he killed his family."

Melissa chewed a mouthful of food. She was consciously trying to calm the panic rising within her.

"His attacks were always strong, though," Melissa blurted. "I mean, they're not getting any stronger than they always were. It's just his visage that is becoming clearer."

"I've thought of that too," Bill said, pointing his chopsticks at her. "But I think it's important that we note that his attacks are becoming more disturbing with time. At least his attacks on you. But, you're the only one there to attack, aren't you?"

Melissa felt herself blush. She was very cognizant of her stubborn stupidity in refusing to leave that house, and yet, she just couldn't bring herself to go.

"That's very true," she said softly. "The attacks are getting more…not violent, but I don't know."

"Intimate," Drema said. Melissa nodded.

They all ate in contemplative silence for the next few minutes until they all heard a car door slam outside. Bill jumped up and walked to the door. Melissa heard voices in greeting and then Bill came into the room with a woman Melissa assumed was his mother. His very stylish mother.

She was a beautiful older woman. She was wearing a light blue cashmere wrap and perfectly pressed khaki slacks and honest-to-God penny loafers. Her soft blonde hair had the look of being windswept, and her makeup was light and expertly applied.

"Melissa, this is Karen McKinney," Bill said. He looked at

the woman expectantly and she smiled at Bill and nodded.

"The witch," Bill said.

Melissa gaped at the woman who smiled back serenely.

"We told you she wasn't what you expected," Drema said.

"I get that a lot," Karen said.

"Karen, this is Melissa Caan," Drema said.

"So you're the poor woman living in Thomas Schaeffer's haunting grounds, hmm?" Karen said, unwrapping herself from the deliciously soft cashmere to show off a simple white silk blouse. "Ooh, can I have that egg roll?"

"Help yourself, please," Drema said.

Bill produced a chair and sat it next to Melissa. Karen sat and began daintily munching on the egg roll. Melissa stared at her, watching as not even the shell of the egg roll dared to soil Karen's lovely clothes. Karen looked over at Melissa and smiled warmly.

"Honey," Karen began. "You look like someone walloped you upside the head with a two-by-four. Am I really that much of a surprise?" Melissa shook herself and cleared her throat.

"I'm so sorry," Melissa said. "I'm being totally rude. Actually I'm feeling just a little bit overloaded here. You see, I'm here to get the ENAPS report on their investigation of my home and there have been some pretty disturbing findings concerning my home. And then I'm told that since my case is so bizarre, I need the help of a witch to clean it out. Yes, you're not what I expected at all, but that's no excuse for me to gawk at you like that."

Karen smiled and reached out and squeezed Melissa's hand.

"Don't you worry about it, honey," Karen said. "We're cool." Melissa laughed.

"Now, Drema my dear, I wonder if I might be brought up to date on Melissa's case?" Karen said. Melissa noticed that Karen was very warm and personable, but there was also an air of authority about her that got people moving. Drema immediately began talking and showing Karen the video. Karen looked over at Melissa a time or two during her briefing, a small frown causing a line to stand out between her perfectly shaped eyebrows.

"Damn," Karen said after Drema had finished. "I know that I'm asked to help on your more complicated cases, but this one sure is scary." Drema and Bill nodded in unison.

"Of course I bought the house with the violent man ghost," Melissa said, feeling suddenly sullen. "I couldn't get the kindly old lady ghost. *No.* Mine had to be a special case."

Karen started laughing and Bill joined her. Drema chanced a sideways grin and a huffy guffaw. Eventually Melissa laughed too, hearing how pouty she sounded. After the giggles had stopped and Karen had carefully wiped the tears from her eyes while avoiding smearing her eye makeup, it was down to business again. Karen needed some time to procure supplies and to do some reading to make sure that the exorcism—Melissa had been shocked that they were calling it an exorcism, always thinking of Linda Blair and green puke at the word—would be successful on the first try. They all agreed to try for no later than that Thursday, and Melissa made her drive to Ida's house (it was almost time for the boys to be back from school) feeling both burdened by the findings of the investigation and lifted by Karen's confidence.

CHAPTER SIXTEEN

Drema called her Tuesday evening on her cell phone as she was eating dinner with Ida and the boys. She excused herself from the table, knowing Ida would demand to be filled in after the boys had gone down. Despite their own experiences and Ryan's (thankfully fading) injury, Melissa had done her best to keep all of this mess hidden from them, telling them that she was having hunters come and find the wild animal that killed Dumb-Dumb. Logan had looked at her suspiciously a couple of times, but had ultimately kept quiet.

"We're coming tomorrow, Melissa," Drema said instead of a formal greeting.

"That was fast," Melissa said.

"Karen knows how dire your situation is," Drema said simply. "I told you you were a priority."

"I believed you," Melissa said. "Thank you so much, Drema. I mean it."

"You keep saying it and I believe you, too," Drema said. "We'll try for noon, while the boys are at school, okay?"

"Sure, sounds good," Melissa said.

When she resumed her seat at the table, Ida cocked an eyebrow at her and Melissa jerked her head to the kids to indicate that she couldn't talk about it just then. The boys finished their dinners and put their plates in the sink and then begged Ida to let them feed Sophie. Ida laughed and led them out back and pointed out the best dandelion greens to pick to feed the goat. She sat on a bench next to Melissa and waited quietly for Melissa to talk.

"They're coming tomorrow," Melissa said.

"Wow, they meant it when they said they'd get it done fast, didn't they?" Ida asked. Melissa nodded.

"Didn't you tell that ex of yours that you'd let him know so he could come keep an eye on you all?" Ida asked. Melissa gasped and smacked the side of her head. She'd completely forgotten.

She pulled out her cell phone and sent Kyle a simple text letting him know. He replied by thanking her and promising to be there. Melissa read his text aloud to Ida and Ida scoffed.

"He wadn't invited," she said sourly. Melissa smiled at Ida.

"You don't like him much, do you?" Melissa asked.

"Aw, it ain't nothin' he's done to me," Ida began. "I've just come to be so fond of you and them boys and I get all pissed at that man for hurtin' you and tearin' up your family like he did."

"But look at me," Melissa said smiling widely and gesturing to herself. "I'm soooo over that man. And I've got a new guy that I need to get away from now!"

"I've been thinking," Ida said, ignoring Melissa's joke. "I know another way you and Liddy are alike."

"Oh?" Melissa said, sitting up.

"She was stubborn like you," Ida said. "That's why she put up with ol' Thomas's bullshit for so long. She was committed and by God she was gonna make it work. You're like that, you know. Look at you, refusing to leave that house just because you ain't gonna back down on a commitment, no matter how dumb or crazy you look. No matter how hurt you might get."

Melissa frowned at Ida.

"Are you calling me dumb?" Melissa said.

"Ain't the first time," Ida said, smiling at her.

"Well hopefully that witch can help tomorrow. Hopefully, I can go back to a normal life after tomorrow," Melissa said.

"I'm gonna be there too," Ida said. Melissa smiled at her.

"I knew I couldn't get rid of you," Melissa said.

"Damn right you ain't," Ida said. "What is this fancy pants witch's name?"

"Karen McKinney," Melissa said. She laughed. "I swear she looks like a senator's wife, not a witch."

"Maybe she does that 'cause she's smart," Ida said. "If you're gonna be anything other than Christian in a town like this, you'd better do it with a low profile." Ida frowned and rubbed her chin. "I think I know her name, though. You think she was about my age?"

Melissa looked at Ida. Ida, with her thin and small frame and shaved head was not exactly a rough-looking woman, but there was something about her that Melissa, if pressed, would have said made Ida look like a tough piece of meat. Jerky, maybe. Karen was an older woman, but she wasn't sure if she and Ida were closer than ten years in age. She told Ida as much and Ida nodded thoughtfully.

"McKinney ain't a rare name 'round here. Lots of 'em. I wish I knew her people before I let her come and do some sort of hocus pocus on your home," Ida said. Melissa knew that Ida was wanting to know Karen's family and not the other witches (if there were any). Knowing a person's family and their history was big with Ida.

"Well you'll meet her tomorrow. Maybe seeing her in person will ring some bells. Maybe not," Melissa said, watching the boys. "Either way, things are getting done. I feel good about it. Cautiously so."

"Cautiously is a good way to approach it. We need to be hopeful, but if things go bad, we don't want to be feeling too let down," Ida said.

The boys got their baths not much later and were sent to bed. Melissa didn't stay long after and went home knowing that Ida would be coming back home with her the next day after the boys had been sent off to the bus. Her night was quiet and uneventful. A small part of her dared to hope that her threat to leave had permanently pacified the spirit of Thomas Schaeffer. She made sure it *stayed* a small part.

When the ENAPS van and another vehicle drove up her driveway the next day, Melissa and Ida were sitting on the front porch, both of them tense and lost in their own thoughts.

"That van's still just the ugliest thing I ever saw," Ida muttered.

A simple blue car parked next to the van. Karen was

driving and she had a passenger with her. The passenger was an extremely tall black woman. Like Ida, her head was shaved, but she wore giant gold earrings and a flowing purple sundress. She was strikingly beautiful. Drema and Bill were helping Karen and her passenger unload a large plastic tote from the trunk. When Melissa noticed that Karen was carrying a cupcake carrier she frowned and looked over at Ida to see if she'd noticed. Ida was still staring at the ENAPS van in annoyance. Melissa smiled and elbowed Ida in the side.

"You don't have to drive it," Melissa said to Ida.

"Thing's as ugly as sin, I don't know why anybody would want to," Ida said.

"I tend to agree," Karen chimed in, climbing the porch steps. "Drema, sweetheart, that van is terribly garish."

Drema actually smiled at Karen.

"But it's great for marketing," Drema answered. "You see that van, you remember it."

"Oh, I never thought of that!" Ida said, laughing heartily.

"That's too brilliant by half," Karen said, laughing herself.

"Yeah, well, Drema also hates change," Bill said. "We had that van personalized when we first started ENAPS twelve years ago and she isn't open to changing it. I mean, you've seen her house, right? No change for this woman."

"It's a comfort thing," Drema said in her simple way. "I like routine and I like for most of my surroundings to be unchanging."

"As is your choice," Karen said, smiling broadly.

"Um, excuse me, but are those cupcakes?" Melissa asked, pointing to the carrier Karen was holding.

"They are!" Karen said brightly. "I like cupcakes and I anticipate that I'll need one after this and I thought I'd make enough for everybody. They're lemon!"

"Well you're in good company," Ida said. "Me and Melissa, we've got healthy appetites. We like to eat."

"The best people do," Karen said.

"Now, I understand you're a McKinney?" Ida asked. Melissa rolled her eyes and smiled apologetically at Karen. Karen waved a hand dismissively and smiled.

"I am. I'm a local girl, born and raised," Karen said. "I know you from high school. You were a senior when I was a freshman at Victory. Your maiden name was Knight, right?"

"That's right," Ida said, surprised.

"Well you probably didn't notice underclassmen too much. None of us did," Karen said. Ida smiled and seemed to relax and Karen winked at Melissa.

"Ladies, let me introduce my plus-one," Karen said, gesturing to the tall woman. "This is my daughter, Freya. She's going to be helping me today. Actually, I'm going to help *her*. She's sensitive to the other side of the veil and she's got a little more experience with malevolent spirits than I do." Karen looked at the politely blank faces of Melissa and Ida, seeming to know that they were wondering about the younger woman's paternity. "I vouch for her entirely," Karen said, smiling proudly.

"Freya is great to work with," Drema said.

"Oh, that's enough gushing," Freya said. She looked down at Melissa. "I've been told of your problem and I'm here to help," she said, smiling. Her teeth were big, but it made her smile sweet and infectious. There was a warmth to her that Melissa yielded to instantly.

"Thank you so much for coming," Melissa said to everyone. "I'm so glad to see an end to all of this. This was supposed to be my fresh start, and it sort of stalled on me."

"I'll say!" Karen said.

"And what kind of payment are you two asking?" Ida asked, pointing and wagging a finger between Karen and Freya. It wasn't delivered rudely, and neither women took it badly.

"Well first of all, we'd appreciate tight lips about us and our involvement," Karen said.

"We enjoy our anonymity," Freya said.

"And secondly, I sure do love apple pie," Karen said, both she and Freya smiling like Cheshire cats.

"You mean, you don't expect payment?" Melissa asked. "I mean, at least let me reimburse you for the supplies. I insist."

"Ugh," Karen said dramatically. "This is such an unpalatable topic of conversation." She put a hand on Melissa's shoulder. "Let's make sure it works before we talk about reimbursement, okay?" she said seriously. Melissa nodded.

Kyle's SUV was coming down the driveway. He parked and walked up onto the porch, and stood close to Melissa.

"Hi, I'm Kyle, her ex-husband," He introduced himself. "Hey, Ida!"

"Hey," Ida said politely.

Karen was looking at Kyle. Her face had gone flinty, but before Kyle could register the coldness in her eyes, they cleared and returned to their blue warmth. She smiled and shook Kyle's hand. Melissa got the impression that Karen was checking Kyle out to make sure he was okay.

"Welcome!" Karen said. "I'm Karen McKinney and this is my daughter, Freya. We're witches and today we're playing the part of the venerable exorcists! And those two lovely people beside my daughter are Drema Farrell and Bill Howarth. They're the only members of the Eastern North American Paranormal Society, or ENAPS as we call them. They're studious investigators and just terrific all-around people."

"Hello!" Kyle said, holding his hand up in greeting.

"Hi," Drema said seriously.

"Nice to meetcha," Bill said, waving back.

"Well if we're all here, I think we should talk about what's going to happen today," Freya said. "Can we go into the house?"

Melissa nodded and gestured for everybody to go in ahead of her. Kyle was first, followed by Ida and Drema and Bill. Freya looked at her mother, smiled and went in. Karen stood before Melissa and looked at her in an oddly serious way.

"You can trust him, he doesn't mean you harm anymore," Karen said. Melissa blinked.

"My threat worked?" Melissa said, shocked.

Karen needed a moment to understand what Melissa was talking about and she started giggling.

"Oh, I'm such an idiot sometimes," she said. "No, I mean your ex-husband. You made the right decision, whatever it was." She got another faraway look in her eyes and she spoke in a dreamy way. "Some people never stop to thank the stepping stone that buries itself in the mud to keep others from getting muck on their boots, and he's one of them. But he will make a good ally."

"How do you know that?" Melissa said, frowning and smiling all at once. Karen just smiled and tapped an index finger on the side of her nose. She walked into the house ahead of Melissa, leaving Melissa alone to shake her head.

"God, I hope this works," Melissa said, walking into her home.

CHAPTER SEVENTEEN

"I haven't opened myself up yet, but man, oh man, can I feel a strong presence in this place," Freya was saying to the group. "What I want to do first is make contact with the spirit. I don't want to come in all prepared for attack when it's possible that this can be resolved in a peaceful and quiet way."

"How would you do that?" Melissa asked.

"As a clairvoyant, I can manipulate the world that the spirit sees. See, I know that Thomas Schaeffer suffered a rather traumatic death, and it's possible that the consciousness within which he exists at this time is skewed. Perhaps if I can remind him of peaceful surroundings and the easy beauty of it all, his eyes might clear and he'd move on," Freya answered.

"I don't want to sound rude, I really don't," Melissa began. "But that sounds completely bonkers." Both Karen and Freya laughed good-naturedly.

"I know that the outside perspective is a bit dubious of what we do," Karen said. "Surely, seeing is believing, though?"

"I have to admit that for some reason, I trust you. Both of you," Melissa said. "I'm trying to be open-minded, especially considering some of the things that have happened to me since I moved into this house. But, can you at least assure me that you've done this before? You're not going to pull out one of those how-to books for dummies, right?" Again, Karen and Freya laughed.

"She's a crack-up, isn't she?" Karen asked the group.

"I don't know how she keeps such a sunny disposition considerin' what she's been through," Ida said fondly.

"She's strong," Karen said. "She heals quick and she makes herself a rock for those she loves." Melissa blushed.

"To answer your question, Melissa, yes I've done this before. I've been aware of this ability of mine since I was seventeen years old and I performed my first cross-over at eighteen. A cross-over is the peaceful resolution. I did my first exorcism at twenty-four. I'm thirty-one years old now and I admit, if there were books for dummies on what I do, I'd probably read them," Freya said. Melissa laughed nervously.

"And if a peaceful resolution isn't going to happen, what then?" Melissa asked.

"Then we do the exorcism," Freya said. "I need to walk around here a bit, but I am getting the impression that the spirit isn't based in this house. What I mean by that is, most spirits have a stronghold. Sometimes it's a particular room, or a place in the yard. It's almost like their spawning point. When they've exhausted themselves, the spirits go away and need to recharge and they always originate anew in this one particular place. They sometimes leave this place or they haunt this one point exclusively, depending on how strong they are. I get the feeling that I need to go out to that barn."

"He was murdered in the barn," Drema said.

"If the barn is his home, then we'll cleanse the house first. We'll drive out all the negativity that lingers here and block him from coming back in," Freya said. "Then we'll go out to the barn and confront the spirit himself and drive him out."

"Usually, we urge the homeowners to stay back and away while we do this," Karen said. "It's distracting having a stressed-out person following you around and trying to talk. But Drema tells us that you are this spirit's focus. He follows you around, even gets in bed with you. We'll need you near not only to keep in his face, but also to protect you."

"Why do I need protecting if you're here?" Melissa asked, shocked.

"Spirits who reject crossing over rarely take an exorcism quietly," Freya said sympathetically.

"So we might be in actual danger here?" Kyle asked, sitting up.

"*You'll* be fine," Karen said coolly. "This spirit likes attacking women and children. As he was in life, in death he is a bully and a coward." Kyle sat back into the couch cushions, looking uneasy. "Now that we've covered some of the basics, Melissa, will you walk with me?" Freya asked, standing. Melissa nodded and stood as well. Freya turned and looked at the rest of the group. "If you'll excuse us," Freya said, smiling politely. She took Melissa's hand like they were old pals and led Melissa into the kitchen. Freya kept hold of Melissa's hand and put her other hand on a wall. Her eyes were closed and Melissa fidgeted uncomfortably.

"What I'm doing right now is called psychometry," Freya said softly. "I'm feeling for energy and trying to gauge a general mood of this place." She paused and looked at Melissa seriously. "There's so much anger in here, Melissa. Not only from the spirit, but from you. I find that so odd. You're being victimized, and it's pissing you off." Freya was speaking as if the new ideas were pouring into her head as she was talking. She smiled as the last sentence left her lips.

"This house and land were my dream for a very long time," Melissa answered. "I needed a new life and I needed to feel in control again. I've been more scared in this house than I have at any other time of my life, but I feel resentful that I couldn't just have the peace and quiet that I wanted so much."

"That's why you refuse to leave. You refuse to feel beaten," Freya said. "Again."

"Yeah," Melissa said quietly. "I guess so."

"Can I see the children's bedrooms, please?" Freya asked, not releasing Melissa's hand. Trying to take it in stride, Melissa led her up the stairs and into Logan's room first. Freya put a hand on the wall.

"Tell me about the dog," Freya said. "The boy who lives in this room has had such sad thoughts about the dog."

"They were outside with the dog, both boys. They said his skin just opened up. They saw it. By the time I got out there, and I was running like hell, the dog was dead. Ida and I both thought that it looked like he'd been cleaved with an axe. It was awful," Melissa said.

"You lied to them," Freya said.

"I told them it was a wild animal that got hold of him," Melissa answered.

"He's mad about it," Freya said.

"Well that's just too bad," Melissa said, feeling indignant. "That story is better than what I think actually happened." Freya opened her eyes and smiled down at Melissa.

"My mom used to say that a lot. *That's too bad*," Freya said. Melissa led her into Ryan's bedroom and Freya did the hand-on-the-wall thing again.

"This is the room of the little one that was attacked?" Freya asked. Melissa nodded.

"He was so scared," Freya said. "He wanted his mommy very much." Melissa bit her lower lip.

They did this in every room of the house, Freya always keeping a grip on Melissa's hand. When they had finished, they returned to where the rest of the group was still sitting in the living room.

"I'll need you for this part, Mom," Freya said. Karen nodded and joined Freya (who was still holding Melissa's hand), and the three walked out of the house and toward the barn. Melissa felt her shoulders start to tense and move up, her heart started beating harder and her mouth was suddenly very dry. Freya released her hand when they got to the giant red door so that Melissa could unlatch it and open it. The sun was out and strong that day and the light poured in through the open door. The barn was silent. Freya resumed her hold on Melissa's hand and Karen walked in behind them. Freya stopped and stared up at the center beam, frowning at it.

"That's where..." Karen began and Freya nodded solemnly.

"Yeah, this is the place where he goes," Freya said. She walked to a wall and put her hand on it. Because they were still holding hands, Melissa felt Freya shiver before she stepped away from the wall, looking at it as if it had said something distasteful to her. She turned to Melissa and smiled suddenly.

"Can I see the little poem that's in the hayloft? Drema told us about it," Freya said. Melissa pointed to the ladder and hoped that she could stay down on the ground level. Freya let go of her hand and climbed the ladder, followed closely by her mother.

Melissa paced the bare floor, listening to the witches' hushed talking in the hayloft. She was trying to focus on the mundane so that she could stand being in the barn alone. She was looking at the feed bins and reminding herself to call the farm supply store to put in a refill order. She was kneeling down and looking at a hole in a wall that looked suspiciously like a mouse hole when the familiar tingle of her hair prickling overcame her. By the time she had stood up straight, she was practically panting in her panic. Her eyes brushed over the cavernous room, looking for the shadow. She exhaled loudly when she saw nothing. She thought that maybe all of this build-up to an exorcism and having witch/exorcists in her house had made her jumpy. Then he whispered in her ear.

"Nobody walks out on me," the voice said.

Before Melissa could yelp in surprise, her right arm was wrenched behind her back painfully and she was slammed into the barn wall face-first. She cried out and heard the frantic movements of the witches behind her.

"Stop it, Thomas," Melissa said, though her cheek was pushed into the wall so hard that her jaw couldn't open. She was shoved harder and her arm was wrenched up higher. She could hear her the ligaments in her shoulder groan like a rubber band about to snap. She screamed.

"MELISSA, LOOK AT ME," Freya was screaming into her face. Melissa hadn't noticed that her eyes had closed. She opened them and looked into the deep brown eyes of the witch, just inches from her own face. Freya's warm hand reached out and put a firm grip on Melissa's wrenched arm. She said nothing, but suddenly Melissa was freed and she fell into Freya, who caught her in an embrace. Karen moved in behind Melissa and Melissa found herself as the meat portion of a surprisingly comforting witch sandwich. She was trying to slow her breathing down and fight the urge to burst into scared, frustrated tears.

"You stop that now," Karen said, stroking Melissa's hair. "If tears need to come, let them."

Melissa stubbornly shook her head on Freya's shoulder.

"It's not weakness, Melissa," Freya said sternly. "Don't you dare think that."

It took a moment for the words to get past the traumatized cloud of thought that permeated Melissa's brain, but when they did get through, Melissa broke down. She cried from the constant fear she tried to hide; she cried from the way she flinched whenever she heard a creak or groan of wood settling inside of her own home; she cried because she couldn't look into Ryan's smiling face without seeing the enormous black bruise on his side; she cried for Dumb-Dumb, whose protective instincts for her and the boys was probably why he was mutilated. Freya and Karen kept her sandwiched between them, providing solid comfort through her weeping. As the flood of emotions started to subside, Melissa became very self-conscious about openly crying in front of two strangers, as well as their closeness. She pulled away slowly, wiping at her face, avoiding the eyes of the two witches. They backed up and gave her the space to put herself back to rights.

"Thank you for helping me," Melissa said, looking at her shoes.

"You needed it," Freya said. "I wasn't just going to stand there and watch."

"Let's get you back to the house," Karen said. Karen grabbed Melissa by the shoulders and turned her towards the door, then both of the witches flanked her and they started walking out of the barn.

"I haven't had anything happen since I threatened to leave. I thought that maybe he was gone, but he told me just then that nobody leaves him. That was the longest he's ever been quiet since I've lived here," Melissa said, not wanting to walk in silence.

"He knows we're here feeling him out," Freya said.

"He feels threatened, maybe?" Melissa asked.

"Maybe," Karen said.

"Then why did he attack me? I mean obviously I don't want you all to get hurt, but why me?" Melissa asked, fully aware of the whiny tone of her voice and not caring.

"You're his impetus," Karen said. "As far as we know,

this place was never considered haunted until you moved in. The workers who built your house? Nothing. The remaining Rhineharts who would come out here to mow the lawn and do upkeep on that barn? Nothing. Nothing like this happened until you moved in, Melissa. He took a shine to you, I guess."

"Well fuck him and the horse he rode in on," Melissa said. "I was never very good at getting the attentions of men, but the ones I do get never seem to go away."

"You remind him of his wife," Karen said simply.

"Why do I keep getting that?" Melissa said, frustrated. "We look nothing alike. Ida keeps saying it's deeper than looks but I don't get it! What, am I going to hear next that I'm Liddy's reincarnation?"

"That would be a coincidence that is just far too convenient," Freya said. "Your spirits are just similar, that's all."

"I don't want this," Melissa said.

"That's why we're here," Karen said, giving Melissa a pinch on her arm.

"I think we can probably go ahead and get started," Freya said. "Melissa, I'm going to try to contact him in the house, where he's not as strong. I'm still going to try to resolve this peacefully and quietly. It's just better for everybody that way." Melissa nodded and led the way up the porch stairs, smiling at the thought of her witch protectors walking tightly beside her the whole way back to the house.

Melissa hustled the group of people seated in her living room to the kitchen where she made them all sandwiches and Ida prepared a large pitcher of iced tea. Ida had given Melissa several worried glances as had Kyle. Melissa was sure her eyes were red and puffy but she was thankful that nobody asked any questions. She was also thankful that nobody was being too pushy about being a spectator. These people were there for her, but they were happy to do it in a quiet and unobtrusive way. When Drema, Bill, Kyle and Ida were settled in the kitchen and Melissa was certain she'd done enough to not seem rude, she went into the living room where Freya was seated on the couch and Karen was sitting on the coffee table before her daughter. Melissa stood back in the hall entryway, trying not to interrupt anything.

"It's best if you come sit with us," Freya said. "You're safer with us close."

"Great," Melissa mumbled. She went into the living room and sat on one of the arm chairs that faced the couch.

"I'm going to take myself to his realm of consciousness," Freya said. "Once there, I'm going to try to communicate to him that he needs to let go of his anger and move on."

"And I need to be here why?" Melissa asked cautiously. Truth be told, she would have rather sat in the kitchen eating sandwiches and chit-chatting with the others.

"He's with you always, Melissa," Karen said sternly. "He's most likely going to be preoccupied with Freya and won't bother you, but just in case he lashes out, you need to be near us so we can stop any attacks before they get too intense."

"This is most likely going to be very boring to you," Freya said softly. "I'm just going to be sitting here looking like I'm meditating, okay? Just take yourself to a calm place and picture yourself surrounded by a big bubble of white light that goes over your head and under your feet and nothing bad can get in. Try to relax, Melissa."

Melissa did as she was told and tried to picture herself in a protective bubble. However, ten minutes into Freya's contact, Melissa found herself bored. Both Karen and Freya were quiet and motionless. Melissa could see only Karen's back, but Freya's eyes were closed and she looked like she was indeed meditating. Another five minutes passed before Freya opened her eyes and blinked at her mother. She had a very sad look on her face and she shook her head slowly.

"We'll do the exorcism, then," Karen said softly.

"I didn't work?" Melissa asked.

"He wouldn't even notice me or anything I did. I manipulated his environment, I tried talking right to him, and nothing. He's so fixated on you and wondering where the kids are. He just stalks around both hating you and fearing you leaving him and wanting to punish you and the kids," Freya said.

"He can't be reasoned with, then," Melissa said.

"No," Freya said, sounding tired. "He is beyond reason."

CHAPTER EIGHTEEN

The entire group had to be present for the exorcism. Karen said it was because they needed the concentrated will of everybody present. Melissa had a moment of doubt when she saw Freya pull a folded piece of notebook paper from one of the plastic totes and look it over. Freya noticed Melissa's startled look and explained that she was just being as careful as possible to make sure this was done absolutely right.

Everybody was given a large feather and told to picture the white bubble as Melissa had been instructed earlier. The witches asked that everybody picture this white bubble following them from room to room and that they use their feathers to sweep out all of the bad energy. The witches looked like pack mules with pouches strapped across their chests. They each held a stick that was about a foot long and had shiny wire wrapped around the bottom ends.

"Are those wands?" Kyle asked.

"These are hawthorn wands," Karen answered. "They're particularly good for exorcisms."

The witches instructed that everybody form a circle on Melissa's front porch. It was dramatic and confusing watching Karen and Freya as they "cast a circle" and begged certain deities that Melissa had never heard of to aid them in their task and keep them safe from "the malicious dead." Everybody stayed silent and reverent toward what was going on, but Melissa knew that Ida and Kyle at the very least were as lost as she was.

"We start from the top of the house and work our way

down. We cleanse this house and drive out all of the negativity and then we go to the barn and cast him out from where he lives," Freya said.

The group went up to Melissa's attic and followed the witches' instructions, waving the feathers in a sweeping motion and moving around the room in a counter-clockwise motion. Karen and Freya were sprinkling what they explained was a mixture of salt and cumin on the floor—they also explained that they'd clean up their mess when the exorcism was complete, to Melissa's delight—to drive out evil. Karen went to all the windows, dabbing small amounts of oil on the window sills and doorways in order to keep anything bad from reentering. When each room had been swept clean by the group, they waited outside of the room as the witches went back into the room and set a small bowl in the center and lit a bundle of dried herbs in order to complete the cleansing. The rooms were left open as they filled with the heavily perfumed scents of the herbs.

When the attic, second floor and most of the first floor, save for the living room, were finished without incident, Melissa felt a huge wave of relief. Maybe she was just buying into the program that the witches were setting up, but she swore that she felt a lightness in the house that hadn't been there before. So when they began on the living room, she was caught completely off guard when she was thrown against the wall and strangled.

Everybody literally dropped everything and rushed to her. Kyle, who was closest, got to her first and she could barely make out the terror on his face as her vision started to fade. The pressure building in her head and behind her eyes was almost as unbearable to her as the fact that her throat was squeezed closed by invisible hands and an invisible body was pressed against her, holding her against the wall. She clawed helplessly at her neck. She could hear Kyle talking to her, saying her name over and over incredibly fast, "LISSLISSLISSLISSLISS," and she tried to look at him, but her eyes were unfocused as her hands picked at the skin on her throat, trying to find a way to let air into her lungs. She heard Karen scream at Kyle. Kyle moved away and Melissa felt Karen press herself against Melissa and whisper into her ear.

She awoke on the floor with Ida kneeling next to her, tears streaking her face. Kyle was a sickly gray color and everybody else simply looked worried.

"There, there, there she is," Karen said softly from behind her. Melissa became aware that her head was resting in Karen's lap. She moved her head back to look into Karen's face and winced at the deep pain in her neck.

"No, don't talk," Freya said.

"How?" Melissa said, wincing at both the pain and the rough sound of her voice. She sat up and accepted a glass of water from Drema. Swallowing hurt. A lot. The coppery taste of the blood in her throat wasn't a holiday, either.

"We finished cleansing this room while Mom protected you. You passed out, and thankfully you could breathe again," Freya answered.

"Thank you," Melissa mouthed, rubbing her throat gingerly.

"That was the scariest fucking thing I've ever seen," Kyle said. Ida nodded in agreement.

"Liss, I really thought you were going to die. Your face turned purple and your eyes were almost completely popped out of your skull," Kyle said.

"You stop that now," Karen said to him. "It stopped and she still lives."

"And your house is cleared," Freya said, smiling at Melissa. She reached out and brushed some hair off of Melissa's sweaty face. "He's not in here anymore and he can't get back in."

Tears were streaming down Melissa's face now. Ida made a pained noise and gathered Melissa into her arms and hugged her fiercely.

"You poor girl," Ida murmured. "You poor, poor girl."

"We're not done yet, though," Freya said. "And you all need to build up your confidence because I'm afraid that this was supposed to be the easy part. Now we do the barn, where he lives."

"Okay," Kyle said. "Let's finish this. On to the big boss fight!" Melissa smiled at him, knowing that that was what he was trying to accomplish. Raw emotions tended to make Kyle uncomfortable, she remembered, and he was always trying to ease tension by making lame jokes.

"Melissa," Karen said, putting her face inches away from Melissa's. "You need to be out there with us so that we can finish this. I won't leave your side even for a second, I promise. Are you up for it? Get your life back on track, bring your boys home, get this dream life going again?"

Melissa nodded, smiled weakly, and gave a thumbs up. Karen smiled and patted Melissa's cheek gently. Ida and Freya put their hands under each of Melissa's arms and helped her stand. Melissa went into the kitchen, put some ice into a plastic Baggie to hold to her throat and nodded at the group in a determined way.

"'Atta girl," Ida said, putting a protective arm around Melissa's waist. Karen came and put an arm over Melissa's shoulder and Melissa made her way to the barn completely boxed in by the two women. They stayed pressed to her, and the rest of the group stayed directly in front of Melissa in an equally protective show. Melissa's face stayed wet from the tears that just wouldn't stop flowing.

Freya opened the barn door and stood aside to let everybody in. Karen nodded at Ida over Melissa's head to indicate that Ida should join the rest of the group. Karen led Melissa to the feed bins and sat Melissa on the floor, sliding down to join her. Melissa spared a thought for Karen's immaculate slacks and how dirty they were getting on the barn floor.

"You just sit and watch," Karen whispered to her. "I'll keep you safe."

Drema, Bill, Kyle and Ida started the sweeping motions with their feathers, starting at the back of the barn and working in a counter-clockwise motion as they'd been instructed to do in the house. Freya plunged a fist into one of the pouches she had slung over herself and started sprinkling the salt and cumin on the floor. She was murmuring softly and all her concentration was bent on this task.

And then suddenly he was there. Standing in the middle of the room directly under the center beam was Thomas Schaeffer. He was no shadow man, nor was he shapeless. One moment, the space was empty, and the next, a tall man stood there looking at

Melissa. Melissa croaked in surprise and started to scramble to her feet, but Karen's hands clamped onto her upper arms.

"Stay put, Melissa," Karen said. "Trust in the ritual and in the people who are here for you. He won't touch you, I swear it." Thomas walked towards her. He was slow but full of purpose, his eyes blazing with anger and malice. Melissa could hear the heavy sounds of his boots as they hit the floor, but when he was within about two feet of her and Karen, a bright white light flashed and Melissa saw the bubble of protection. She looked over and Karen, was glaring back at the apparition, who was looking perplexed. He lifted a hand and pointed at Melissa and disappeared. Drema started screaming.

All eyes darted to the source of the pained screams and Melissa saw Drema falling to the ground. Bill tried to catch her but fell into a tangled heap with her instead. Melissa started to get up to go to her, but Karen's vice-like grip on her arm kept her seated. Melissa looked over at Karen and she simply shook her head, telling Melissa that she couldn't leave the circle.

"She's bleeding!" Bill screamed. Freya and Ida were kneeling beside Drema, and Kyle had pulled out his phone.

"NO!" Drema said, looking at Kyle. "Just wait a minute, will you?"

"You're bleeding all over the place!" Kyle said incredulously. "You need an ambulance!"

"I'll need medical attention for sure, but it's not life-threatening and it scared me more than anything. Come here, look at it," Drema said. Kyle knelt down with everybody else. The entire group had ashen complexions and pursed lips.

"Tell me," Karen said to the group. They all looked up to Melissa and Karen. Melissa felt her chest tighten. These people were all terrified.

"She's been grazed," Freya said. "She'll need stitches and she's going to have a horrible bruise, but her pants took most of the abuse."

"What happened?" Melissa asked.

"It looks like she was swiped with some sort of blade," Bill said. "A knife or something."

"Or an axe," Ida said.

"Yeah," Bill agreed.

"Coward," Freya said. "You only attack women and children, is that it? The helpless are the most attractive recipients of your abuse?"

"Freya," Karen said. Freya looked at her mother for a moment before lowering her eyes. The four remaining group members helped move Drema so that she was sitting on the other side of Karen, presumably inside of the circle of protection that Karen was working so hard to maintain. Drema's face had gone a greenish-gray color and her lips were pale. Sweat was beading on her forehead and her hair was sticking to her neck and temples. Melissa leaned over to put a hand on Drema's forearm and Drema gave Melissa a weak smile. Melissa glimpsed at the gash on Drema's thigh. Her black pants had split cleanly and there was a three-inch-long gash in the meaty part of the leg. It wasn't bleeding profusely and Melissa was glad that the femoral artery had been missed.

"It hurts," Drema said. "Like the blade was hot or something. The cut hurts, but the burning is what's driving me crazy."

"I've got something for that," Karen mumbled, watching the standing members of their group as they resumed the cleansing ritual.

Freya was still throwing handfuls of the cumin and salt all over the floor. She would glance up every second or two at the center beam, making Melissa wonder what it was that she saw up there. Melissa was listening to Drema's panting through the pounding of her own heart. She could feel a great amount of soft warmth emanating from Karen and she found herself leaning on the older woman, seeking the creature comfort of her body. Karen put an arm around Melissa in a motherly and protective way, watching Freya carefully.

Thomas was there again. There was no coming or going with him. He was suddenly there or suddenly gone. He was standing under the center beam, his arms crossed over his chest, the long handle of the axe resting on one of his legs, the head by one of his heavy boots. He was watching Freya, but he glanced over his shoulder at Melissa and glared at her. Melissa jerked upright and meant to yell to Freya, but Karen held her back again.

"Freya is more than capable of protecting herself. Don't worry about her," Karen said into Melissa's ear.

"Ida, then," Melissa said, knowing Bill and Kyle had no reason to fear bodily harm from Thomas.

"Take care, ladies," Karen said. Freya turned and looked at Thomas. She turned and looked at Ida then walked to her and took her hand. She nodded to Bill and Kyle to continue with what they were doing and dragged Ida gently by the hand as she scattered her salt mixture and herbs, chanting under her breath the whole time. Ida had a shocked, frightened look on her face. She would look every now and then at the apparition of the man standing in the center of the room, the axe displayed at his side.

Melissa was watching the strange circular dance that Freya seemed to be doing around Thomas, avoiding him, but moving closer to him at every rotation. Melissa noticed that she was swaying lightly with Karen, who was mouthing words quietly with her daughter. That's why Melissa screamed when Thomas was suddenly kneeling before her, looking into her face. She jerked backwards hard into Karen's side, making Karen grunt in surprise and pain. Thomas's eyes flicked to Karen and his mouth slowly formed a word.

"Mine."

He started to reach out for Melissa, and Karen's grip on Melissa's arm tightened to the point of pinching pain. Melissa sank back into Karen, trying to have faith in the circle of protection. When the ghost's hand touched the barrier and it flashed into being, he disappeared. Melissa had filled her lungs with air; she let out a sigh of relief then she was jerked out of Karen's grip and thrown to the middle of the room. She hit the bare board with a crash, her face smashing down. Her vision was blackened by her nose breaking on the fall. She sat up, holding her face, feeling the wet blood start to run over her upper lip in a warm stream. She wiped at it and bounced around all over the floor, trying to locate her attacker. Karen was scrambling to her, crawling along the floor, ruining her once immaculate slacks. Melissa held her arms out to Karen, reaching for her when she was jerked to a standing position by strong hands around her throat. By the way the fingers wrapped around her windpipe, she knew she was being held from behind. Karen and Freya were standing in front of her, hands outstretched, screaming words that got lost in the haze of her own panic. Her head hurt from the busted nose, she was choking on blood running down her throat, her throat (still sore from being choked earlier) was screaming from the current grip, and her feet weren't touching the floor.

She opened her eyes and tried to focus on a face. She saw Kyle. Her mouth moved, but no sound could come out.

"Take care of my babies," she mouthed at him as best as she could, hoping he could make it out. Thomas was going to kill her and take her with him, and she knew it. As long as she was the only one to go, she was at peace with that being the way to get rid of him.

"Don't you dare, damn it!" Ida screamed at her. Her voice cut through the pain and the air being squeezed from Melissa's body. Melissa focused on the waving and flailing tiny frame of Ida Conklin.

"Don't you give up, girl!" Ida screamed at her. "You think of them boys! They need their mother, you hear me? Don't you close your eyes!"

Melissa tried to grip the hand closed around her throat, but again there was nothing there. She began to struggle, to try to break free. She reached out for the witches. Ida was thrown to the ground with a shout. She stood up, her mouth bloody.

"I been hit before, you sumbitch!" she screamed in Melissa's direction. "You ain't takin' this girl like you did Liddy and Dave and Donna! You ain't killin' again, you bastard!"

The witches paused in their chanting and they turned and looked at Ida. Ida's eyes were aflame with purpose. She walked closer. She walked past the witches, who were watching her in surprise. She stopped just in front of Melissa. The grip on Melissa's throat had let up just enough for Melissa to wheeze enough air into her lungs to keep from passing out. Ida was looking up and past Melissa's face, glaring.

"Liddy weren't no cheater," Ida said. "And them kids was good kids, better than you deserved, you drunken, useless, petty piece of garbage. The Rhineharts knew Liddy was too good for you. You killed the best parts of yourself when you killed your family, Thomas Schaeffer, and them boys comin' out here and draggin' you up that beam with a chain was exactly what you had comin' to you!"

Melissa was shaken by the neck by the phantom hands holding her above the floor. Her neck popped painfully and she almost wished that he would kill her to stop the agony. Tears were running down her face and she saw Ida flick a worried glance at her. The witches had continued their chanting behind Ida.

"Liddy took them kids away and never came back after you killed 'em. You lost. They're gone. SHE LEFT YOU," Ida screamed above Melissa's head.

Melissa was dropped onto the floor. She gasped, painfully drawing air into her lungs, crying at the anguish in her throat. Kyle and Bill rushed in and pulled her up and dragged her to the wall by the feed bins. She turned in their grasp and looked on. There was Ida, the tiny tough woman, standing toe to toe with the ghost before her, both of them glaring at each other.

"For every bit of mean you threw at her, for every attempt to control and imprison her, Liddy still got away. You been alone now, all these sixty-some years. This woman," Liddy pointed to Melissa and Thomas turned his head and looked at her. "She ain't Liddy. Liddy's gone. You need to go too, damn it. This ain't your place no more."

Thomas was in front of Melissa again. He reached for her. Bill and Kyle both wrapped their arms around her protectively, but Melissa had had enough. Her throat hurt, her nose was still bleeding, her entire body ached and hurt. She jerked herself out of the men's grip and walked closer to the ghost. She had to spit out a thick gob of blood that was blocking air from going cleanly through her throat. She stood on her tiptoes to stare into his eyes, noticing they were not solid—she could see the rest of the barn through him. He looked back steadily, angrily.

"Go," she croaked at him, pointing towards the door. Her voice wasn't working and it came out as a rough whisper.

The ghost's face started to wrinkle up into a snarl. She

started to doubt the sense in standing up to him and prepared to be hit, but it never came. He disappeared, but the whole barn rang out with a deafening scream of rage so severe that if it had come from a human throat, it would have surely been as shredded as Melissa's was at the moment. When the barn was again silent, the two witches sandwiched Melissa between them, forming a circle around her with their arms.

"It's not over yet, honey, but almost," Karen said to her.

Angels of Earth, spirits of light
Aid us in our exorcism fight.
Evil spirits take leave of this home
Peaceful halls of man you no longer roam.
Your body swallowed by the Earth
Your spirit holds no hope of rebirth.
By the gods of the Earth, air and light
You are compelled to depart and set things right.
You are banished from our sight forever more
Imprisoned by the hatred that rotted your core.
Be gone now, never to return
Hope that the powers above don't set you to burn.
Peace on this home and those living within
Let a new time of happiness for all begin.

The witches repeated the incantation several times. There was much banging and stomping by heavy boots. A man was heard huffing and bellowing. Finally, they all heard a loud crack and all eyes settled on that center beam moments before it split in two right at the mark where the chain had dragged across and fell to the floor with a frightening crash. Melissa looked from the ruin of her barn floor to the faces of those around her. While Drema, Bill, Ida, and Kyle all huddled on the floor together looking pale and scared to death, the witches were smiling at each other, panting and perspiring.

"And that's that," Freya said.

"Huh?" Melissa croaked voicelessly.

"It is done," Karen said.

CHAPTER NINETEEN

Drema needed stitches (though she said she was in much less pain after Karen had put some sort of poultice on the wound), and Melissa was given X-rays to make sure that nothing in her neck was broken. Her nose was reset and she was given a prescription for some particularly lovely, warmth-inducing pain pills. The doctor at the ER was unhappy with their group for not giving explanations as to what had happened to the two women. He gave Ida and her bruised mouth a sidelong glance and glared at Kyle and Bill.

His attitude softened slightly when Karen, who had been administering lemon cupcakes to their battered party (which also included Logan and Ryan, who had gotten back to Ida's just in time for the hospital trip) and the nurses, pressed a cupcake into his own hand. He huffed loudly and left the room with his confection.

Melissa didn't let the boys move back into the house until two weeks had passed without incident. The light feel of the atmosphere that she had detected in the house proved to be real and once she accepted it as permanent reality, she brought her sons home. Their excitement for their home was alighted anew as if it were moving day all over again. They were happy to be reunited with their toys and surrounded by the things that represented the memories of their family. Ida cried when they left, but she got into her car and followed them and stayed with Melissa until after midnight. She kissed Melissa on the forehead when she left and told Melissa that she loved her. Melissa returned the sentiment and hugged Ida.

They burned the barn the weekend after the boys came home. Karen and Freya returned and finished the cleansing inside before "the holla' boys," as Ida called them, set the barn ablaze. They were really just fellow residents of the hollow who were happy to help one of their own. They grilled hamburgers for everybody, and even Drema, Bill and Kyle showed up to watch the red barn burn and fall in on itself. Every physical memory of Thomas Schaeffer, his murders and his own death, were erased from Melissa's brand spankin' new home.

The next weekend, the holla' boys came back and helped to bury the remains of the old barn. Melissa cooked a large pan of lasagna as a thank you and sent everybody home with half of an apple pie. She really liked be a part of a small community that didn't give a second thought to helping someone.

Drema helped Melissa find out where Liddy, David, and Donna were buried and even drove with Melissa to the cemetery. Melissa laid flowers on their graves and cried while Drema stood beside her with a supportive hand on her shoulder. Melissa didn't care much for walking to the other side of the cemetery to see where Thomas was buried. She was so glad to be rid of his spirit that the thought of being near his mortal remains made her sick to her stomach and phantom pains in her throat flared up.

Melissa had a prefabricated aluminum barn put on the property where the old barn had stood. When its cookie-cutter glory was completed, she hosted a big pig roast and invited everybody she knew. One of the holla' boys had a son who had a bluegrass band. They set up in Melissa's yard and played well into the night for an eclectic mix of people celebrating. One of the holla' boys, a man named Kevin Bennett, produced a canning jar of moonshine and insisted they have a toast to spirits departed. When they all had their red Solo cups containing a shot of moonshine held high, Kevin made his toast.

"To those who called this land home who went before us! Here's to you, Three-Notch-Axe Holla'. Now that ol' Tom's gone, maybe we'll have us a good year!"

All plastic cups were raised and drained followed by some

whoops and coughs. Melissa stood smiling to herself. She cornered Ida and poked a finger into the small woman's face.

"You could have told me about Threenechex meaning Three-Notch-Axe," Melissa said to her. Ida just smiled at Melissa.

"Somethin' big like what happened here in 1954 don't go away without some sort of commemoration. The boys started callin' it Three-Notch-Axe not long after ol' Thomas died 'cause of some rumor that he put three notches in that big ol' axe of his after he killed his family. One fer each life he took. The name got muddied and we started saying it fast so as to blur up some of the meaning, but that's how this holla' got its name, girl. Threenechex Holla'."

"That's sick," Melissa said, smiling and shaking her head.

"Yeah, but it's part of the holla' fabric now. Get used to it," Ida said, patting her cheek and walking away.

About the Author

Somer Canon is a minivan revving suburban mother who avoids her neighbors for fear of being found out as a weirdo. When she's not peering out of her windows, she's consuming books, movies, and video games that sate her need for blood, gore, and things that disturb her mother.

Curious about other Crossroad Press books?
Stop by our site:
http://store.crossroadpress.com
We offer quality writing
in digital, audio, and print formats.

CPSIA information can be obtained
at www.ICGtesting.com
Printed in the USA
BVHW041833170919
558653BV00015BA/428/P